IN HIS
STEPS

IN HIS STEPS

CHARLES M. SHELDON

SPIRE

© 1984 by Chosen Books

Published by Revell
a division of Baker Publishing Group
P.O. Box 6287, Grand Rapids, MI 49516-6287
www.revellbooks.com

New Spire edition published 2012

ISBN 978-0-8007-8608-3

Printed in the United States of America

Scripture is taken from the King James Version of the Bible.

16   17   18   7   6   5   4

Foreword

In His Steps by Charles M. Sheldon has been challenging readers to a spiritual adventure now for over eighty-five years. Behind the writing of this book is a fascinating story. Dr. Sheldon was the pastor of the Central Congregational Church in Topeka, Kansas. One hot June afternoon in 1896, the minister decided to try an unusual kind of sermon for his Sunday night services. He would write a continued story, one chapter to be given each week about what happened in the lives of various persons, with different backgrounds and vocations, who applied to every decision the question "What would Jesus do?"

Dr. Sheldon was soon preaching to a packed church with standing room only. Young people especially crowded these Sunday evening services.

When the series was over, the story was published as a serial in the *Advance*, a weekly religious paper in Chicago. It was then offered to three different publishers. All turned it down. Finally the *Advance* put it out in a ten-cent paperback edition. Over 100,000 copies of this edition were sold in a matter of weeks.

The amazing part of the story followed. Because the *Advance* had sent only a portion of the manuscript to the Copyright Office in Washington DC, the copyright was later declared invalid. Thus, because it belonged to the public domain, sixteen publishers in the United States were soon printing it. The editions then spread around the world—England, France, Germany, Norway, Russia, Bulgaria, on to Greece and India—in the end, forty-five countries. There is no way of knowing the total number of copies sold and the numbers of lives touched by the challenge of Jesus's way of life. A conservative estimate would be over 30 million copies of *In His Steps* distributed, the world's record next to the Scriptures.

Although Dr. Sheldon realized almost no royalty from these remarkable sales, that fact never made him bitter. He felt that the defective copyright had been turned by God to unprecedented good. *In His Steps*, carefully edited and updated for modern readers, remains today as timely as it was when first published so many years ago.

The Publishers

1

It was Friday morning, and the Reverend Henry Maxwell was trying to finish his Sunday morning sermon. He had been interrupted several times and was growing nervous as the morning wore away and the sermon grew very slowly toward a satisfactory finish.

"Mary," he called to his wife as he went upstairs after the last interruption, "if anyone comes after this, I wish you would say that I am very busy and cannot come down unless it is something very important."

"All right, Henry. But I am going over to visit the kindergarten, and you will have the house all to yourself."

The minister went up into his study and shut the door. In a few minutes he heard his wife go out, then everything was quiet.

He settled himself at his desk with a sigh of relief and began to write. His text was from 1 Peter 2:21: "For even hereunto were ye called: because Christ also suffered for us, leaving us an example, that ye should follow his steps."

He had emphasized in the first part of the sermon the atonement as a personal sacrifice, calling attention to the fact of Jesus's suffering in various ways in His life as well as in His death. He had then gone on to emphasize the atonement from the side of example, giving illustrations from the life and teaching of Jesus, to show how faith in Christ helped to save men because of the patterns or character He displayed for their imitation. He was now on the third and last point, the necessity of following Jesus in His sacrifice and example.

He had just put down "Three steps: what are they?" and was about to enumerate them in logical order when the doorbell rang sharply.

Henry Maxwell sat at his desk and frowned a little. He made no movement to answer the bell. Very soon it rang again. Then he rose and walked over to one of his windows that commanded a view of the front door.

A man was standing on the steps. He was a young man, very shabbily dressed.

"Looks like a tramp," said the minister. "I suppose I'll have to go down, and—"

He did not finish his sentence, but went downstairs and opened the front door.

There was a moment's pause as the two men stood facing each other. Then the shabby-looking man said, "I am out of a job, sir, and thought maybe you might give me a lead toward something."

"I don't know of anything. Jobs are scarce," replied the minister, beginning to shut the door slowly.

"I didn't know but that you might perhaps be able to give me a lead to the railroad office or the plant superintendent or something," continued the young man, shifting his faded hat nervously from one hand to the other.

"It would be of no use. You will have to excuse me. I am very busy this morning. I hope you will find something. Sorry I can't give you something to do here, but I do the work myself."

The Reverend Henry Maxwell closed the door and heard the man walk down the steps. As he went up into his study, he saw from his window that the man was going slowly down the street, still holding his hat between his hands. There was something in the figure so dejected, homeless, and forsaken that the minister hesitated a moment as he stood there at the window. Then he turned to his desk, and with a sigh began the writing where he had left off.

He had no more interruptions. When his wife returned two hours later, the sermon was finished, the loose leaves gathered up and neatly tied together and laid on his Bible, all ready for the Sunday morning service.

"A queer thing happened at the kindergarten this morning, Henry," said his wife while they were eating dinner. "You know I went over with Mrs. Brown to visit the school, and just after the games, while the children were at the tables, the door opened and a young man came in, holding a dirty hat in both hands. He sat down near the door and never said a word, only looked at the children. He was evidently a tramp, and Miss Wren and her assistant, Miss Kyle, were a little frightened at first. But he sat there very quietly, and after a few minutes he went out."

"Perhaps he was tired and wanted to rest somewhere,

Mary. The same man called here, I think. Did you say he looked like a tramp?"

"Yes, very dusty and shabby. Probably in his early thirties, I should say."

"The same man," said the Reverend Henry Maxwell thoughtfully.

"Did you finish your sermon, Henry?" his wife asked, after a pause.

"Yes, all done. It has been a very busy week with me. The two sermons have cost me a good deal of labor."

'What are you going to preach about in the morning?"

"Following Christ. I take up the atonement under the head of sacrifice and example, and then show the steps needed to follow His sacrifice and example."

"I am sure it is a good sermon. I hope it won't rain Sunday. We have had so many stormy Sundays lately."

"Yes, I'm afraid people will not come out to church in a storm." Pastor Henry Maxwell sighed as he said it. He was thinking of the careful, laborious efforts he had made in preparing sermons for large audiences that failed to appear.

On Sunday the town of Raymond had one of the perfect days that sometimes come after long periods of wind and rain and mud. The air was clear and bracing, the sky free from all threatening signs. When the service opened at eleven o'clock, the large building was filled with an audience of the best-dressed, most comfortable-looking people in Raymond.

The First Church of Raymond believed in having the best music money could buy, and its quartet choir this morning was a source of great pleasure to the congregation. The

10

anthem was inspiring. All the music was in keeping with the subject of the sermon. And the anthem was an elaborate adaptation to the most modern music of the hymn:

> Jesus, I my cross have taken
> All to leave and follow thee.

Just before the sermon, the soprano, Rachel Winslow, sang the well-known hymn:

> Where He leads me I will follow
> I'll go with Him, with Him, all the way.

Rachel looked very beautiful that morning as she stood up behind the screen of carved oak that was significantly marked with the emblems of the cross and the crown. Her voice was even more lovely than her face, and that was saying a great deal.

There was a general rustle of expectation over the audience as she rose. Mr. Maxwell settled himself contentedly behind the pulpit. Rachel Winslow's singing always helped him. He generally arranged for a song before the sermon. It made possible a certain inspiration of feeling that he knew made his delivery more impressive.

People said to themselves that they had never before heard such singing, even in the First Church. It is certain that if it had not been a church service, her solo would have been vigorously applauded. It even seemed to the minister when she sat down that something like an attempted clapping of hands or a striking of feet on the floor swept through the church. He was startled by it. As he rose, however, and laid his sermon on the Bible, he said to himself that he had been deceived. Of course it could not occur. In a few moments he was absorbed in his sermon and everything else was forgotten in the pleasure of his delivery.

No one had ever accused Henry Maxwell of being a dull preacher. On the contrary, he had often been charged with being sensational—not in what he said so much as in his way of saying it. But the First Church people liked that. It gave their preacher and their parish a pleasant, agreeable distinction.

It was also true that the pastor of the First Church loved to preach. He was eager to be in his own pulpit when Sunday came. That was an exhilarating half-hour for him as he faced a church full of people and knew that he had a hearing. He was peculiarly sensitive to variations in the attendance. He never preached well before a small audience. The weather also affected him decidedly. He was at his best before just such an audience as faced him now, on just such a morning. He felt a glow of deep personal satisfaction as he went on. The church was the first in the city. It had the best choir. It had a membership composed of the leading people, representatives of the wealth, society, and intelligence of Raymond.

He was going abroad on a two-month vacation in the summer, which reflected the circumstances of his pastorate, his influence, and his position as pastor of the first church of the city.

The sermon was interesting. It was full of striking sentences which would have commanded attention if printed. Spoken with the passion of a dramatic utterance that had the good taste never to offend with ranting or declamation, it was very effective. If the Reverend Henry Maxwell that morning felt satisfied with the conditions of his pastorate, the First Church also had a similar feeling as it congratulated itself on the presence in the pulpit of this scholarly, refined, somewhat striking face and figure, preaching with such animation and freedom from all vulgar, noisy, or disagreeable mannerism.

Suddenly into the midst of this perfect accord and concord between preacher and audience came a remarkable interruption. It would be difficult to indicate the extent of the shock which this interruption measured.

The sermon had come to a close. Mr. Maxwell had just turned half of the big Bible over onto his manuscripts and was about to sit down, as the quartet prepared to rise to sing the closing selection:

> All for Jesus, all for Jesus,
> All my being's ransomed powers.

Suddenly the entire congregation was startled by the sound of a man's voice. It came from the rear of the church. The next moment the figure of a man came out of the last row of seats and walked down the middle aisle.

Before the startled congregation fairly realized what was going on, the man had reached the open space in front of the pulpit and had turned about, facing the people.

"I'm not drunk and I'm not crazy, and I'm perfectly harmless," he began. "But if I die, as there is every likelihood I shall in a few days, I want the satisfaction of thinking that I said my say in a place like this and before this sort of crowd."

Mr. Maxwell had not taken his seat, and he now remained standing, leaning on his pulpit, looking down at the stranger. Before him was the man who had come to his house the Friday before—the same dusty, worn, shabby-looking young man. He held his faded hat in his hands. It seemed to be a favorite gesture. He had not shaved, and his hair was rough and tangled. It was doubtful if anyone like this had ever before confronted the congregation and pastor of First Church.

There was nothing offensive in the man's manner or tone. He was not excited, and he spoke in a low but distinct voice. Mr. Maxwell was conscious, even as he stood there smitten into dumb astonishment at the event, that somehow the man's action reminded him of a person he had once seen walking and talking in his sleep.

No one in the church made any motion to stop the stranger or in any way interrupt him. Perhaps the first shock of his sudden appearance deepened into genuine perplexity concerning what was best to do. However that may be, he went on as if he had no thought of interruption and no thought of the unusual element he had introduced into the decorum of the First Church service. And all the while he was speaking the minister leaned over the pulpit, his face growing more white and sad every moment. But he made no movement to stop him, and the people sat smitten into breathless silence. One other face, that of Rachel Winslow from the choir, stared white and intent down at the shabby figure with the faded hat. Her face was striking at any time. Under the pressure of the present incident, it was as personally distinct as if it had been framed in fire.

"I'm not an ordinary tramp, though I don't know of any teaching of Jesus that makes one kind of a tramp less worth saving than another. Do you?" He put the question as naturally as if the whole congregation had been a small Bible class. He paused just a moment and coughed painfully. Then he went on.

"I lost my job ten months ago. I am a printer by trade. The new linotype machines are beautiful specimens of inventions, but I know six men who have killed themselves inside of the year just on account of those machines. Of course, I don't blame the newspapers for getting the machines. Meanwhile, what can a man do? I know I never learned but my one trade, and that's all I can do. I've tramped all over the country trying to find something. There are a good many others like me. I'm not complaining, just stating facts. But I was wondering, as I sat here in church this morning, if what you call following Jesus is the same thing as what He taught. What did He mean when He said, 'Follow me'?"

Here the man turned about and looked up at the pulpit. "Your minister said that it was necessary for the disciple of Jesus to follow His steps, and he said the steps were obedience, faith, love, and imitation. But I did not hear him tell you just what he meant that to mean, especially the last step. What do you Christians mean by following the steps of Jesus? I've tramped through this city for three days trying to find a job, and in all that time I've not had a word of sympathy or comfort except from your minister here, who said he was sorry for me and hoped I would find a job somewhere. I suppose it is because you get so imposed on by the professional tramp that you have lost your interest in the other sort. I'm not blaming anybody, am I? Just stating facts.

"Of course, I understand you can't go out of your way to hunt jobs for people like me. I'm not asking you to, but what I feel puzzled about is, what is meant by following Jesus? What do you mean when you sing, 'I'll go with Him, with Him, all the way'? Do you mean that you are suffering and denying yourselves and trying to save lost, suffering humanity just as I understand Jesus did? What do you mean by it? I see the ragged edge of things a good deal. I understand there are more than five hundred men in this city just like me. Most of them have families. My wife died four months ago. I'm glad she is out of trouble. My little girl is staying with a printer's family until I find a job. Somehow I get puzzled when I see so many Christians living in luxury and singing, 'Jesus, I my cross have taken, all to leave and follow thee . . .' and remembering how my wife died in a New York tenement gasping for air and asking God to take the little girl, too.

"Of course I don't expect you people can prevent everyone from dying of starvation, lack of proper nourishment, and tenement air, but what does following Jesus mean? I understand that Christian people own a good many of the tenements. A member of a church was the owner of the one where my wife died. I have wondered if following Jesus all the way was true in his case. I heard some people singing at a church prayer meeting the other night,

> All for Jesus, all for Jesus;
> All my being's ransomed powers;
> All my thoughts and all my doings,
> All my days and all my hours.

"I kept wondering as I sat on the steps outside just what they meant by it. It seems to me there's an awful lot of trouble in the world that somehow wouldn't exist if all the people who sing such songs went and lived them out. I suppose I don't understand. But what would Jesus do? Is that what you mean by following His steps? It seems to me sometimes as if people in the big churches have good clothes and nice houses to live in and money to spend for luxuries, and can go away on summer vacations and all that, while the people outside the churches, thousands of them, I mean, die in tenements and walk the streets for jobs, and never have a piano or a picture in the house, and grow up in misery and drunkenness and sin."

The man gave a queer lurch over in the direction of the Communion table and laid one grimy hand on it. His hat fell upon the carpet at his feet. A stir went through the congregation, but as yet the silence was unbroken by any voice or movement. The man passed his other hand across his eyes, and then, without any warning, fell heavily forward on his face.

Henry Maxwell said, "We will consider the service closed." He was down the pulpit stairs and kneeling by the prostrate form before anyone else. The audience instantly rose and the aisles were crowded.

Dr. Philip West was the second to reach the inert figure and pronounced the man alive. "He seems to have a heart problem," the doctor muttered as he helped carry him to the pastor's study.

2

Henry Maxwell and a group of his church members remained some time in the study. The man, whose name they discovered was Jack Manning, lay on the couch there breathing heavily. When the question of what to do with him came up, the minister insisted upon taking the man to his house. He lived nearby and had an extra room.

Rachel Winslow said, "Mother has no company at present. I am sure we would be glad to give him a place with us." She looked strangely agitated. No one noticed it particularly. They were all excited over the strange event, the strangest that First Church people could remember.

But the minister insisted on taking charge of the man, and when a carriage came, the unconscious form was carried to his house. With the entrance of that humanity into the minister's spare room, a new chapter in Henry Maxwell's life began. Yet no one, himself least of all, dreamed of the remarkable change it was destined to make in his Christian discipleship.

The event created a great sensation in the First Church parish. People talked of nothing else for a week. It was the general impression that Jack Manning had wandered into the church in a condition of mental disturbance caused by his troubles, and that all the time he was talking he was in a strange delirium of fever and really ignorant of his surroundings. It was the general agreement also that there was a singular absence of anything bitter or complaining in what Manning had said. He had spoken throughout in a mildly apologetic tone, almost as if he were one of the congregation seeking for light on a very difficult subject.

Throughout the week after his removal to the minister's house there was little change in Jack Manning's condition. Saturday morning he began to fail and Dr. West was called. When the physician arrived, Jack Manning rallied for a while and asked to see his daughter.

"Your child is coming," Mr. Maxwell said, his face showing marks of the strain of the week's vigil. The minister had found the daughter's address through some letters in Manning's pocket and had sent for her.

"I shall never see her in this world," Jack whispered. Then he uttered with great difficulty the words, "You have been good to me. Somehow I feel as if it was what Jesus would do." After a few moments he turned his head slightly, and before Mr. Maxwell could realize the fact, the doctor said quietly, "He's gone."

Sunday morning dawned on the city of Raymond exactly as it had the Sunday before. Mr. Maxwell entered his pulpit to face one of the largest congregations that had ever crowded First Church. He was haggard and looked as if he had just risen from a long illness. His wife was at home with the little girl, who had arrived several hours after her father had died. The minister could see Jack Manning's face as he opened the Bible and arranged his different notices on the lectern as he had been in the habit of doing for ten years.

The service that morning contained a new element. No one could remember when Henry Maxwell had preached in the morning without notes. As a matter of fact, he had done so occasionally when he first entered the ministry, but for a long time he had carefully written every word of his morning sermon and nearly always his evening discourse as well. It cannot be said that his sermon this morning was impressive. He talked with considerable hesitation. It was evident that some idea struggled in his thought for utterance, but it was not expressed in the theme he had chosen for his preaching. It was near the close of his sermon that he began to gather a certain strength that had been painfully lacking at the beginning. He closed the Bible and, stepping out at the side of the lectern, faced his people and began to talk to them about the remarkable scene of the week before.

"Our brother"—somehow the words sounded a little strange coming from his lips—"passed away yesterday afternoon. I have not yet had time to learn all his history. He had one sister living in Chicago. I have written her and have not yet received an answer. His little girl is with us and will remain for a time."

He paused and looked over the congregation. He thought he had never seen so many earnest faces during his entire pastorate. How was he to tell his people about the crisis through which he was even now moving?

"The appearance and words of this stranger in church last Sunday made a powerful impression on me," the pastor continued. "I am not able to conceal from you, or myself, the fact that what he said, followed by his death in my house, has compelled me to ask as I never asked before, 'What does following Jesus mean?'"

He stopped a moment, struggling for the right words. "What Jack Manning said her last Sunday was a challenge to Christianity as it is practiced in our churches. I have felt this with increasing emphasis every day this past week. And I do not know that any time is more appropriate than right now for me to propose to you the plan that has been forming in my mind as an answer to the stranger's challenge to us."

Again Henry Maxwell paused and looked into the faces of his people. There were some strong, earnest men and women in the First Church. He could see Edward Norman, editor of the Raymond *Daily News*. He had been a member of First Church for ten years. No man was more honored in the community.

There was Alexander Powers, superintendent of the railroad yards in Raymond, a typical railroad man, one who had been born into the business. There sat Donald Marsh, president of Lincoln College, situated in the suburbs of Raymond. Milton Wright was one of the important businessmen of Raymond, having in his employ hundreds of men in various plants.

There was Dr. Philip West, who, although still comparatively young, was quoted as an authority in special surgical cases. And young Jasper Chase. He was the author who had written one successful book and was said to be at work on a new novel.

There was Miss Virginia Page, an attractive heiress in her thirties who, through the recent death of her father, had inherited a million at least. A statuesque blonde of attractive proportions, Virginia had an appealing face. The spectacles she wore simply emphasized her gifted intellect. And not least of all, Rachel Winslow, whose youthful brunette beauty this morning seemed to bring a radiance to the whole choir.

This congregation was indeed blessed with many important and attractive people, Henry Maxwell noted. But as he watched their faces this morning, he wondered how many of them would respond to the strange proposition he was about to make. He continued slowly, taking time to choose his words carefully.

"What I am going to propose now is something which ought not to appear unusual or at all impossible of execution. Yet I am aware that it will be so regarded by a large number of the members of the church. But in order that we may have a thorough understanding of what we are considering, I will put my proposition very plainly, perhaps bluntly. I want volunteers from First Church who will pledge themselves earnestly and honestly for an entire year not to attempt anything without first asking the question, 'What would Jesus do?'"

He stopped again as if he expected some kind of response. There was none. Every eye was fixed intently on the pastor.

"After asking that question of yourself, each of you will follow Jesus exactly as he knows how, no matter what the results may be. I will, of course, include myself in this company of volunteers and shall take for granted that the members of my church here will not be surprised at my future conduct as based upon this standard of action and will not oppose whatever is done if they think Christ would do it. At the close of the service I want all those members who are willing to join such a company to meet in the lecture room, and we will talk over the details of the plan.

"To sum it up, we who volunteer will attempt to follow Jesus's steps as closely and as literally as we believe He taught His disciples to do. We will pledge ourselves for an entire year, beginning with today, so to act."

Henry Maxwell paused again and looked out over his people.

It is not easy to describe the sensation that such a simple proposition apparently made. Men glanced at one another in astonishment. It was not like their pastor to define Christian discipleship in this way. There was evident confusion of thought over his proposition. It was understood well enough, but there was apparently a great difference of opinion as to the application of Jesus's teaching and example.

He calmly closed the service with a brief prayer. The organist began his postlude immediately after the benediction and the people began to file out. There was a great deal of conversation. Animated groups stood all over the church, discussing the minister's proposition.

When the church sanctuary had emptied, Henry Maxwell bade goodbye to several visitors at the front entrance and entered the lecture room. He was almost startled to see that there were perhaps fifty present. Among them Rachel

Winslow and Virginia Page, Mr. Norman, President Marsh, Alexander Powers, Milton Wright, Dr. West, and Jasper Chase.

The pastor closed the door of the lecture room, then went and stood before the little group. His face was pale and his lips trembled with emotion. No man can tell until he is moved by the divine Spirit what he may do, or how he may change the current of a lifetime of fixed habits of thought, speech, and action. Henry Maxwell did not yet know himself all he was passing through, but he was conscious of a great upheaval in his definitions of Christian discipleship, and he was moved with a depth of feeling he could not measure as he looked into the faces of these men and women.

He first asked them all to pray with him. "Lord, we are here to begin an adventure with You. We come very uncertain about the future but with total trust that you will guide and direct us step by step. . . ."

Almost with the fist syllable he uttered there was a distinct presence of the Spirit felt by them all. As the prayer went on, this presence grew in power. They all felt it. The room was filled with it as plainly as if it had been visible. When the prayer closed there was a silence that lasted several moments. All heads were bowed. Henry Maxwell's face was wet with tears. If an audible voice from heaven had sanctioned their pledge to follow the Master's steps, not one person present could have felt more certain of the divine blessing. And so the most serious movement ever started in the First Church of Raymond was begun.

"We all understand," said he, speaking very quietly, "what we have undertaken to do. We pledge ourselves to do everything in our daily lives after asking the question, 'What would Jesus do?', regardless of what may be the result to us. Sometime I shall be able to tell you what a marvelous change has come over my life within a week's time. I cannot now. But the experience I have been through since last Sunday has left me so dissatisfied with my previous definition of discipleship that I have been compelled to take this action. I did not dare begin it alone. I know that I am being led by the hand of divine Love in all this. The same divine impulse must have led you also. Do we understand fully what we have undertaken?"

"I want to ask a question," said Rachel Winslow, her lovely eyes alive with excitement. "I am a little in doubt as to the source of our knowledge concerning what Jesus would do. Who is to decide for me just what He would do in my case. It is a different age. There are many perplexing questions in our civilization that are not mentioned in the teachings of Jesus. How am I going to tell what He would do?"

"There is no way that I know of," replied the pastor, "except as we study Jesus through the medium of the Holy Spirit. You remember what Christ said, speaking to His disciples about the Holy Spirit:

> Howbeit, when he, the Spirit of truth is come, he shall guide you into all the truth; for he shall not speak from himself; but what things soever he shall hear, these shall he speak: and he shall declare unto you the things that are to come. He shall glorify me; for he shall take of mine and shall declare it unto you. All things whatsoever the Father

hath are mine: therefore said I that he taketh of mine and shall declare it unto you.

John 16:13–15

"There is no other test that I know of. We shall all have to decide what Jesus would do after going to that source of knowledge."

"What if others say of us, when we do certain things, that Jesus would not have done it the same way?" asked the superintendent of railroads.

"We cannot prevent that. But we must be absolutely honest with ourselves. The standards of Christian action cannot vary in most of our acts."

"And yet what one church member thinks Jesus would do, another refuses to accept as his possible course of action. What is to render our conduct uniformly Christlike?" asked President Marsh.

Mr. Maxwell was silent some time. Then he answered: "No, I don't know that we can expect that. But when it comes to a genuine, honest, enlightened following of Jesus's steps, I cannot believe there will be any confusion either in our own minds or in the judgment of others. We must be free from fanaticism on the one hand and too much caution on the other. If Jesus's example is the example for the world, it certainly must be feasible to follow it. But we need to remember this great fact. After we ask the Spirit to tell us what Jesus would do and have received an answer to it, we are to act regardless of the results to ourselves. Is that understood?"

All the faces in the room were raised toward the minister in solemn assent. As he studied the faces, Henry Maxwell saw no opposition.

They remained a little longer talking over details and asking questions, and agreed to report to one another the result of their experiences in following Jesus this way in a weekly meeting. Henry Maxwell prayed again. And again the Spirit made Himself manifest. Every head remained bowed a long time. They went away in silence. There was a feeling that prevented speech. The pastor shook hands with them all as they went out. Then he went into his own study room back of the pulpit and knelt. He remained there alone for nearly half an hour.

Though he sensed a change in his own life, Henry Maxwell did not realize that a movement had begun that would lead to the most remarkable series of events that the city of Raymond had ever known.

3

Edward Norman, editor of the Raymond *Daily News*, sat in his office Monday morning and faced a new world of action. He had made his pledge in good faith to do everything after asking, "What would Jesus do?" At the time of his decision, he thought his eyes were open to all possible results. But as the regular life of the paper started on another week's rush of activity, he confronted it with a degree of hesitation and a feeling nearly akin to fear.

Arriving at his office earlier than usual, he sat at his desk in a growing thoughtfulness. He had yet to learn, with all the others in that little company which pledged to do the Christ-like thing, that the Spirit of Life was moving in power through his own life as never before. He rose and shut his door and then did what he had not done for years. He knelt down by his desk and prayed for the divine Presence to direct him.

Then he arose with the day before him, opened his door and began the routine of the office work. The managing editor had just come in and was at his desk in the adjoining room.

One of the reporters there was pounding out something on a typewriter.

Edward Norman began an editorial. The *Daily News* was an evening paper and Norman usually completed his editorial before nine o'clock.

Norman was one of those newspapermen who keep an eye on every detail of the paper. The managing editor always consulted his chief in matters of both small and large importance. Sometimes, as in this case, it was merely a nominal inquiry.

"Yes—no. Let me see it."

He took the typewritten matter just as it came from the telegraph editor and ran over it carefully. Then he laid the sheets down on his desk and did some very hard thinking.

"We won't run this today," he said finally.

The managing editor was standing in the doorway between the two rooms. He thought he had perhaps misunderstood his boss.

"What did you say?"

"Leave it out. We won't use it."

"But—" The managing editor was dumbfounded. He stared at Norman as if the man were out of his mind.

"I think, Clark, that it ought not to be printed, and that's the end of it," said Norman, looking up from his desk.

Clark seldom had any disagreements with the chief. Norman's word had always been law in the office, and he had seldom been known to change his mind. The circumstances now, however, seemed to be so extraordinary that Clark could not help expressing himself.

"Do you mean that the paper is to go to press without a word of the prize fight in it?"

"Yes, that's what I mean."

"But it's unheard of. All the other papers will print it. What will our subscribers say? Why, it's simply—" Clark paused, unable to find words to say what he thought.

Norman looked at Clark thoughtfully. The managing editor was a member of a church of a different denomination from that of Norman's. The two men had never talked together on religious matters, although they had been associated on the paper for several years.

"Come in here a minute, Clark, and shut the door," said Norman.

Clark came in and the two men faced each other alone. Norman did not speak for a minute. Then he said abruptly: "Clark, if Christ were editor of a daily paper, do you honestly think he would print three columns and a half of a prize fight?"

"No, I don't suppose He would."

"Well, that's my only reason for shutting this account out of the news. I have decided not to do anything in connection with the paper for a whole year that I honestly believe Jesus would not do."

Clark could not have looked more amazed if the chief had suddenly gone crazy. In fact, he did think something was wrong, although Mr. Norman was one of the most unlikely men in the world, in his judgment, to lose his mind.

"What effect will this new policy have on the paper?" he finally managed to ask in a faint voice.

"What do you think?" asked Norman, with a keen glance.

"I think it will simply ruin the paper," replied Clark promptly. He was gathering up his bewildered senses and beginning to remonstrate. "Why, it isn't feasible to run a paper nowadays on any such basis. It's too ideal. The world isn't ready for it. You can't make it pay. Just as sure as you live, if you shut out this prize fight report you will lose hundreds of subscribers. It doesn't take a prophet to say that. The very best people in town are eager to read it. They know it has taken place, and when they get the paper this evening they will expect half a page at least. Surely you can't afford to disregard the wishes of the public to such an extent. It will be a great mistake if you do, in my opinion."

Norman sat silent a minute. Then he spoke gently but firmly.

"Clark, what in your honest opinion is the right standard for determining conduct in our world today? Would you not say that the highest, best law for a man to live by was contained in asking the question 'What would Jesus do?', and then doing it regardless of results? In other words, do you not think that men everywhere ought to follow Jesus's example as closely as they can in their daily lives?"

Clark looked embarrassed and moved uneasily in his chair before he answered the editor's question.

"Why, yes—I suppose if you put it on the grounds of what they ought to do, there is no other better standard of conduct. But to succeed in the newspaper business we have got to conform to the customs and recognized methods of society. We can't do as we would do in an ideal world."

"Do you mean that we can't run the paper strictly on Christian principles and make it succeed?"

"Yes, that's just what I mean. It can't be done. We'll go bankrupt in thirty days."

Norman did not reply at once. He was very thoughtful.

"We shall have occasion to talk this over again, Clark. Meanwhile, I think we ought to understand each other. I have pledged myself for a year to do everything connected with the paper after answering the question 'What would Jesus do?' as honestly as possible. I shall continue to do this in the belief that not only can we succeed, but that we can succeed better than we ever did."

Clark rose. "The report does not go in?"

"It does not. There is plenty of good material to take its place, and you know what it is."

Clark hesitated.

"Are you going to say anything about the absence of the report?"

"No, let the paper go to press as if there had been no such thing as a prize fight yesterday."

Clark walked out of the room to his own desk feeling as if the bottom had dropped out of everything. He was astonished, bewildered, excited, and considerably enraged. His great respect for Norman checked his rising indignation and disgust, but with it all was a feeling of growing wonder at the sudden change of motive which had entered the office of the *Daily News* and threatened, as he firmly believed, to destroy it.

Before noon every reporter, pressman and employee on the *Daily News* was informed of the remarkable fact that the paper was going to press without a word in it about the famous prize fight of Sunday. The reporters were astonished beyond measure at the announcement of the fact. Everyone in the composing rooms had something to say about the unheard-of omission. Two or three times during the day when Mr. Norman had occasion to visit the composing rooms, the men stopped their work or glanced around their cases looking at him curiously. He knew that he was being observed strangely but said nothing, and did not appear to note it.

There had been several changes in the paper suggested by the editor, but nothing marked. He was waiting, and thinking deeply. He felt as if he needed time and considerable opportunity for the exercise of his best judgment in several matters before he answered his ever-present question in the right way. It was not because there were not a great many things in the life of the paper that were contrary to the Spirit of Christ that he did not act at once, but because he was yet honestly in doubt concerning what action Jesus would take about them.

When the *Daily News* came out that evening, it carried to its subscribers a distinct sensation. The presence of the report of the prize fight could not have produced anything equal to the effect of its omission. Hundreds of men in the hotels and stores downtown, as well as regular subscribers, eagerly opened the paper and searched it through for the account of the great fight. Not finding it, they rushed to the newsstands and bought other papers. Even the newsboys had not all understood the fact of the omission. One of them was calling out, "*Daily News*! Full 'count great prize fight. *News*, sir?"

A man on the corner of the avenue close by the *News* office bought the paper, looked over its front page hurriedly and then angrily called the boy back.

"Here, boy! What's the matter with your paper? There is no prize fight here! What do you mean by selling old papers?"

"Old papers, nuthin'!" replied the boy indignantly. "Dat's today's paper. What's de matter wid you?"

"But there's no account of any prize fight here! Look!"

The man handed back the paper and the boy glanced at it hurriedly. Then he whistled, while a bewildered look crept over his face. Seeing another boy running by with papers, he called out, "Say, Sam, lemme see your pile!" A hasty examination revealed the remarkable fact that all the copies of the *News* were silent on the prize fight.

"Here, give me another paper—one with the prize fight account!' shouted the customer. He received it and walked off, while the two boys remained, comparing notes and lost in wonder at the event. "Someone slipped a cog at the *News* for sure," said the first boy. But he couldn't tell why and rushed over to the *News* office to find out.

There were several other boys at the delivery room equally upset. The angry remonstrances hurled at the clerk back of the long counter would have driven anyone else to despair. He was used to it, however, and maintained an impassive front.

Mr. Norman was just coming downstairs on his way home, and he paused as he went by the door of the delivery room and looked in.

"What's the matter here, George?" he asked the clerk as he noted the unusual confusion.

"The boys say they can't sell any copies of the *News* tonight because the prize fight isn't in it," replied George, looking curiously at the editor as so many of the employees had done during the day.

Mr. Norman hesitated a moment, then walked into the room and confronted the boys.

"How many papers are there here, boys? Count them out and I'll buy them all."

There was an excited counting of all the papers by these boys.

"Give them their money, George, and if any of the other boys come in with the same complaint, buy their unsold copies. Is that fair?" he asked the boys, who were smitten into unusual silence by the unheard-of action on the part of the editor.

"Fair? Well, I should think so. But will you keep doing dumb things like leaving out prize fights?"

Mr. Norman smiled slightly, but he did not think it was necessary to answer the question. He walked out of the office and went home. On the way he could not avoid that constant query, "Would Jesus have done it?" It was not so much with reference to this last transaction as to the entire motive that had urged him on since he had made the promise. The newsboys were necessarily sufferers through the action he had taken. Why should they lose money by it? They were not to blame. He was a rich man and could afford to put a little brightness into their lives if he chose to do it. He believed as he went on his way home that Jesus would have done either what he did or something similar with the newsboys in order to maintain justice.

He was not deciding these questions for anyone else but for his own conduct. He was not in a position to dogmatize, and he felt that he could answer only with his own judgment and conscience as to his interpretation of his Master's probable action. The falling off in the sales of the paper he had, in a measure, foreseen. But he was yet to realize the full extent of the loss to his newspaper, if such a policy were continued.

4

During the week Edward Norman received numerous letters commenting on the absence from the *News* of the account of the prize fight. Two or three of these letters may be of interest.

Editor of the News:

Dear Sir: I have been thinking for some time to change my paper. I want a journal that is up to the times, progressive, and enterprising, supplying the public demand at all points. The recent freak of your paper in refusing to print the account of the famous contest at the Resort has decided me finally to change my paper. Please discontinue it.

Very truly yours

(Here followed the name of a businessman who had been a subscriber for many years.)

Dear Ed: What is this sensation you have given the people of your burg? What new policy have you taken up? Hope you don't intend to try the "reform business" through the avenue of the press. It's dangerous to experiment much along that line. Take my advice and stick to the enterprising modern methods you have made so successful for the

News. The public wants prize fights and such. Give it what it wants and let someone else do the reforming.

Yours

(Here followed the name of one of Norman's old friends, the editor of a daily in an adjoining town.)

My dear Mr. Norman:

I hasten to write you a note of appreciation for the evident carrying out of your promise. It is a splendid beginning and no one feels the value of it better than I do. I know something of what it will cost you, but not all.

Your Pastor,

Henry Maxwell

One letter that he opened immediately after reading this from Maxwell revealed to him something of the loss to his business that possibly awaited him.

Mr. Edward Norman,

Editor of the *Daily News*:

Dear Sir: At the expiration of my advertising limit you will do me the favor not to continue as you have done heretofore. I enclose check for payment in full and shall consider my account with you closed after that date.

Very truly yours,

(Here followed the name of one of the largest dealers in tobacco in the city. He had been in the habit of inserting a column of conspicuous advertising and paying a very large price for it.)

Norman laid this letter down thoughtfully, and then after a moment he took up a copy of his paper and looked through the advertising columns. There was no connection implied in the tobacco merchant's letter between the omission of the prize fight and the withdrawal of the advertisement. But he could not avoid putting the two together. In point of fact, he afterward learned that the tobacco dealer withdrew his advertisement because he had heard that the editor of the *News* was about to enter upon some queer reform policy that would be certain to reduce its subscription list.

But the letter directed Norman's attention to the advertising phase of his paper. He had not considered this before. As he glanced over the columns, he could not escape the conviction that his Master could not permit some of them in his paper. What would He do with the paper's advertisements of choice liquors and cigars?

As a member of a church and a respected citizen, he had incurred no special censure because the liquor interests advertised in his columns; no one thought anything about it. It was all legitimate business. Why not? Raymond enjoyed a system of easy licenses, and the saloon and the pool hall and the beer garden were a part of the city's daily life. He was simply doing what every other businessman in Raymond did. And it was one of the best-paying sources of revenue. What would the paper do if he cut these out? Could it live? That was the question. But—was that the question after all?

"What would Jesus do?" That was the question he was answering, or trying to answer, this week. Would Jesus advertise whisky and tobacco in His paper?

Edward Norman asked it honestly, and after a prayer for help and wisdom he asked Clark to come into the office.

Clark came in feeling that the paper was at a crisis and prepared for almost anything after his Monday morning experience. This was Thursday.

"Clark," said Norman, speaking slowly and carefully, "I have been looking at our advertisements and have decided to dispense with certain ones when the contracts run out. I wish you would notify the advertising agent not to solicit or renew the ads I have marked here."

He handed the paper with the marked places over to Clark, who took it and looked over the columns with a serious air.

"This will mean a great loss to the *News*. How long do you think you can keep this sort of thing up?" Clark was astonished at the editor's action and could not understand it.

"Clark, do you think if Jesus were the editor and proprietor of a daily paper in Raymond He would print advertisements of whisky and tobacco in it?"

"Well—no, I don't suppose He would. But what has that to do with us? We can't do as He would. Newspapers can't be run on any such basis."

"Why not?" asked Norman quietly.

"Why not! Because they will lose more money than they make, that's all." Clark spoke out with irritation. "We shall certainly bankrupt the paper with this sort of business policy."

"Do you think so?" Norman asked the question not as if he expected an answer, but simply as if he were talking with himself. After a pause he said, "You may direct Marks to do as I said. I believe it is what Jesus would do, and as I told you, Clark, that is what I have promised to try to do for a year regardless of what the results may be to me. There are some other advertisements of a doubtful character I shall study, too. Meanwhile, I feel a conviction in regard to these that cannot be silenced."

Clark went back to his desk feeling enraged and alarmed. He was sure that the paper would be ruined as soon as it became generally known that the editor was trying to do everything by such an impractical moral standard. What would become of business if this standard were adopted? It would upset every custom and introduce endless confusion. It was simply foolishness. It was downright idiocy, so Clark said to himself; and when Marks was informed of the action, he seconded the managing editor with some very forcible exclamations. What was the matter with the chief? Was he insane? Was he going to bankrupt the whole business?

But Edward Norman had not yet faced his most serious problem.

When he came down to the office Friday morning, he was confronted with the usual plan for the Sunday morning edition. The *News* was one of the few evening papers to issue a Sunday edition, and it had always been remarkably successful financially. There was an average of one page of literary and religious items to thirty or forty pages of sports, theatre, gossip, fashion, society, and political material. This made a very interesting magazine of all sorts of reading matter and it had always been welcomed by all his subscribers as a Sunday morning necessity.

Edward Norman now put to himself the question, "What would Jesus do?" If He were editor of a paper, would He deliberately plan to put into the homes of all the church people of Raymond such a collection of reading matter on the one day of the week that ought to be given up to something better and holier? He was, of course, familiar with the regular argument for the Sunday paper: that the public needed it, especially the working men who would not go to church anyway, and who ought to have something entertaining and instructive on Sunday, their only day of rest. But suppose the Sunday morning paper did not pay? Suppose there was no money in it? How eager would the editor or the proprietor be then to supply this crying need of the working men?

Edward Norman communed honestly with himself over the subject. Taking everything into account, would Jesus edit a Sunday morning paper whether it paid or not? That was not the question. As a matter of fact, the Sunday *News* paid so well that it would be a direct loss of thousands of dollars to discontinue it. Besides, the regular subscribers had paid for a seven-day paper. Had he any right now to give them anything less than what they had paid for?

He was honestly perplexed by the question. So much was involved in the discontinuance of the Sunday edition that for the first time he almost declined to be guided by the standard of Jesus's probable action. He was sole proprietor of the paper. It was his to shape as he chose. He had no board of directors to consult as to policy. But as he sat there surrounded by the usual quantity of material for the Sunday edition, he reached some definite conclusions. And among them was the determination to call in the force of the paper and frankly state his motive and purpose.

He sent word to Clark for the clerical staff, reporters, plant foreman, and those men already at work in the composing rooms, to come into the mailing room. This was a large room, and the curious men came in and perched around on the tables and counters. It was a very unusual proceeding, and they all watched Mr. Norman intently as he spoke.

"I called you in here to let you know my future plans for the *News*. I propose certain changes that I believe are necessary. I understand that some things I have already done are regarded by you men as very strange. I wish to state my motive in doing what I have done." Then he told the men what he had already told Clark, and they stared as he had done and looked as painfully upset.

"Now, in acting on this standard of conduct, I have reached a conclusion that will, no doubt cause some surprise. I have decided that the Sunday morning edition of the *News* shall be discontinued after next Sunday's issue. I shall state in that issue my reasons for discontinuing. In order to make up to the subscribers the amount of reading matter they may suppose themselves entitled to, we can issue a double number on Saturday, as is done by many evening papers that make no attempt at a Sunday edition.

"I am convinced that from a Christian point of view, more harm than good has been done by our Sunday morning paper. I do not believe that Jesus would be responsible for it if He were in my place today. It will occasion some trouble to arrange the details caused by this change with the advertisers and subscribers. That is for me to look after. The change itself is one that will take place. So far as I can see, the loss will fall on myself. Neither the reporters nor the pressmen need make any particular changes in their plans."

He looked around the room and no one spoke. He was struck for the first time in his life with the fact that in all the years of his newspaper life he had never had the workforce of the paper together in this way. "Would Jesus do that?" he thought to himself. "This is, would He run a newspaper on some basis where editors, reporters, pressmen and all could meet to discuss and devise and plan for the making of a paper that should have in view—"

He caught himself drawing away from the facts of typographical unions and office rules and reporters' enterprise, and all the cold, businesslike methods that make a great daily successful. But still, the vague picture that came up in the mailing room would not fade away when Norman had gone back into his office and the men had returned to their places with wonder in their looks and questions of all sorts on their tongues.

Clark came in and had a long serious talk with his chief. He was thoroughly roused, and his protest almost reached the point of resigning his position. Norman guarded himself carefully. Every minute of the interview was painful to him, but he felt more than ever the necessity of doing the Christlike thing. Clark was a valuable man. It would be difficult to fill his place. But he was not able to give any reasons for continuing the Sunday paper that answered the question "What would Jesus do?"

"It comes to this, then," said Clark finally. "You will bankrupt the paper in thirty days. We might as well face that future fact."

"I don't think we shall. Will you stay by the *News* until it is bankrupt?" asked Norman with a strange smile.

"Mr. Norman, I don't understand you. You are not the same man this week that I knew before."

"I don't know myself either, Clark. Something remarkable has caught me up and borne me on. But I was never more convinced of final success and power for the paper. You have not answered my question. Will you stay with me?"

Clark hesitated a moment and finally said yes. Norman shook hands with him and turned to his desk. Clark went back into his room stirred by a number of conflicting emotions. He had never before known such an exciting and mentally disturbing week, but he felt now as if he were connected with an enterprise that might at any moment collapse and ruin him and all connected with it.

Sunday morning dawned again on Raymond, and Henry Maxwell's church was again crowded. Before the service began, Edward Norman drew the curious and thoughtful eyes of most of the congregation. He sat quietly in his usual place about three seats from the pulpit. The Sunday morning issue of the *News* contained the statement of its discontinuance had been expressed in such remarkable language that every reader was struck by it.

The events connected with the *News* were not all. People were eagerly talking about the strange things done during the week by Alexander Powers at the railroad yards, and Milton

Wright in his stores on the avenue. As the service began, there was an undercurrent of excitement in the pews.

Henry Maxwell faced it all calmly. His prayers were filled with hope. His sermon was not so easy to describe. How would a minister preach to his people if he came before them after an entire week of asking himself, "How would Jesus preach?"

It is certain that he did not preach as he had done two Sundays before. Tuesday of the past week he had stood by the grave of the dead stranger and said the words, "Earth to earth, ashes to ashes, dust to dust," and still he was moved by the spirit of a deeper impulse than he could measure as he thought of his people and yearned for the power to preach adequately Christ's message when he was in his pulpit again.

Now that Sunday had come and the people were there to hear, what would the Master tell them? He agonized over his preparation for them and yet he knew he had not been able to fit his message into his ideal of the Christ. Nevertheless, no one in the First Church could remember ever having heard such a sermon before. There was definite rebuke of the greed of wealth and the selfishness of fashion, two things that First Church had never heard rebuked. Yet there was also a love of his people that gathered new force as the sermon went on. When it was finished there were those who were saying in their hearts, "The Spirit moved that sermon."

Then Rachel Winslow rose to sing; this time after the sermon, at Henry Maxwell's request. Rachel's singing did not provoke a rustle of applause this morning. What deeper feeling carried the people's hearts into a reverent silence and tenderness of thought? Rachel was subtly different. Her consciousness of her own loveliness had always marred her singing for those who had the deepest spiritual feeling. It also prevented her from rendering certain kinds of music effectively. Today this vanity was all gone. There was no lack of power in her fine voice. The added elements were of humility and purity distinctly felt by the audience.

Before the service closed, Mr. Maxwell asked those who had remained the week before to stay again for a few moments of consultation, and he also invited any others who were willing to make the pledge. When he was at liberty, he went into the lecture room. To his astonishment it was almost filled. This time a large proportion of the young people had come. But among them were a few businessmen and officers of the church.

As before, he asked them to pray with him. And, as before, a distinct answer came from the presence of the Holy Spirit. The parishioners remained some time to ask questions and consult together. There was feeling of fellowship such as they had never known in their church membership. Mr. Norman's action was well understood by them all, and he answered several questions.

"What will be the probable result of your discontinuance of the Sunday paper?" asked Alexander Powers, who sat next to him.

"I don't know yet. I presume it will result in a falling off of subscriptions and advertisements. I anticipate that."

"Do you have any doubts about your action? I mean, do you regret it or fear it is not what Jesus would do?" asked Mr. Maxwell.

"Not in the least. But I would like to ask for my own satisfaction, if anyone of you here thinks Jesus would issue a Sunday morning paper?"

No one spoke for a minute. Then Jasper Chase said, "We seem to think alike on that, but I have been puzzled several times during the week to know just what He would do."

"I have that trouble," said Virginia Page. Everyone who knew Virginia Page was wondering how she would succeed in keeping her promise in regard to her money. "Our Lord never owned any property nor had much money. There is nothing in His example to guide me in the use of mine. I am studying and praying. I think I see clearly a part of what He would do, but not all."

"I could tell you what to do with part of it," said Rachel, turning her face toward Virginia.

"That does not trouble me," replied Virginia with a slight smile. "What I am trying to discover is a principle that will enable me to come the nearest possible to His action as it ought to influence the entire course of my life so far as my wealth and its use are concerned."

"That will take time," said the minister slowly. All the rest in the room were thinking hard about the same thing.

Then Milton Wright told something of his experience. He was gradually working out a plan for his business relations with his employees and it was opening up a new world to him and to them.

A few of the young men told of special attempts to answer the question. There was also general agreement over the fact that the application of the Christ-Spirit and practice to everyday life was a serious step. It required a knowledge of Him and an insight into His motive that most of them did not yet posses.

When they finally adjoined after a silent prayer, they went away discussing earnestly their difficulties and seeking light from one another.

Rachel Winslow and Virginia Page went out together. Edward Norman and Milton Wright became so interested in their mutual conference that they walked on past Norman's home and came back together. Jasper Chase and the president of the Endeavor Society stood talking earnestly in one corner of the room. Alexander Powers and Henry Maxwell remained even after the others had gone.

"I want you to come down to the railroad yards tomorrow and talk to the men," the superintendent said to his pastor. "Somehow I feel as if you could get nearer to them than anyone else just now."

"I don't know about that, but I will come," replied Mr. Maxwell a little sadly. How was he fitted to stand before two or three hundred working men and give them a message? Yet in the moment of his weakness as he asked the question, he rebuked himself for it. What would Jesus do? That was the end to the discussion.

The next morning Henry Maxwell arrived at Mr. Powers' office a few minutes before twelve. The superintendent said, "Come upstairs and I'll show you what I've been trying to do."

They went through the machine shops, climbing a long flight of stairs, and entered a large, empty room. It had once been used by the company for a storeroom.

"Since making that promise a week ago, I have had a good many thoughts," said the superintendent. "And among them is this: The company gives me the use of this room, and I am going to furnish it with tables and a coffeemaker in the corner there where those steam pipes are. My plan is to provide a good place where the men can come up and eat their noon lunch and give them, two or three times a week, the privilege of a fifteen minutes' talk on some subject that will be a real help to them in their lives."

Maxwell looked surprised and asked if the men would come for any such purpose.

"Yes, they'll come. After all, I know the men pretty well. They are intelligent working men. But they are, as a whole, entirely removed from all church influence. I asked, 'What would Jesus do?', and among other things it seemed to me He would begin to act in some way to add more physical and spiritual comfort to the lives of these men. It is a very little thing, this room and what it represents, but I acted on the first impulse to do the first thing that appealed to my good sense, and I want to work out this idea. I want you to speak to the men when they arrive in a few minutes. I have asked them to come up and see this place and I'll tell them something about it."

Maxwell was ashamed to say how uneasy he felt at being asked to speak a few words to a group of machinists. How could he speak without notes? He shrank from the ordeal of confronting such a crowd, so different from the Sunday audiences with which he was familiar.

There were a dozen long, crude benches and tables in the room. When the noon whistle sounded, the men poured upstairs from the machine shop below and seated themselves at the tables and began to eat their lunches. There were 300 of them. They had read the superintendent's notice, which he had posted up in various places, and came largely out of curiosity.

It was easy to tell from the looks on their faces that they were favorably impressed. The room was large and airy, free from smoke and dust, and well warmed from the steam pipes.

At twenty minutes to one Mr. Powers spoke to them simply, like one who understands thoroughly the character of his audience. Then he introduced the Reverend Henry Maxwell of the First Church, his pastor.

Maxwell never forgot his feelings as he confronted that craggy-faced audience of working men. Like hundreds of other ministers, he had never spoken to any gathering except those made up of people in his own class. This was a strange world to him, and nothing but his new way of life could have given any impact to his message. He spoke on the subject of satisfaction with life, what caused it, what its real sources were. He had the great good sense on this, his first appearance, not to recognize the men as a class distinct from himself. He did not use the term "working men," and did not say a word to suggest any difference between their lives and his own.

The men were pleased. A good many of them shook hands with him before going back to their work, and the minister, telling it all to his wife when he reached home, said that he was surprised how much he enjoyed mingling with these earthy men. The day marked an important one in his Christian experience, more important than he knew. It was the beginning of a fellowship between him and the working world. It was the first plank laid down to help bridge the chasm between the church and labor in Raymond.

Alexander Powers went back to his desk that afternoon much pleased with his plan and seeing much help in it for the men. He knew where he could get some good tables from an abandoned eating house at one of the stations down the road, and he saw how the coffee arrangement could be made a very attractive feature. The men had responded even better than he anticipated, and the whole thing could not help being of great benefit to them.

He took up the routine of his work with a glow of satisfaction. After all, he said to himself, he wanted to do as Jesus would.

It was nearly four o'clock when he opened one of the company's long envelopes, which he supposed contained orders for the purchasing of stores. He ran over the first page of typewritten matter in his usual quick, businesslike manner before he saw that what he was reading was not intended for his office, but for the head of the freight department.

He turned over a page mechanically, not meaning to read what was not addressed to him, but before he knew it, he was in possession of evidence that proved conclusively that the company was engaged in a systematic violation of the interstate commerce laws of the United States. It was as distinct and unequivocal a breaking of law as if a private citizen should enter a house and rob the inmates.

The discrimination shown in rebates was in total contempt of all the statutes. Under the laws of the state it was also a distinct violation of certain provisions recently passed by the legislature to prevent railroad trusts. There was no question that he had in his hand evidence sufficient to convict the company of willful, intelligent violation of the law of the Commission and the law of the state also.

He dropped the papers on his desk as if they were poison, and instantly the question flashed across his mind, "What would Jesus do?" He tried to shut the question out. He tried to reason with himself by saying it was none of his business. He had known in a more or less definite way that such violations had been going on with nearly all the railroads. Indeed, such was known to most officers of the company. Owing to his place in the plant however, he was not in a position to come in contact with the freight operation and had regarded it as a matter that did not concern him. The papers now before him revealed the entire affair. Through carelessness they had been addressed to him. What business was it of his?

Yet if he saw a man entering his neighbor's house to steal, would it not be his duty to inform the officers of the law? Was a railroad company such a different situation? Was it under a different rule of conduct so that it could rob the public and defy law and be undisturbed because it was such a big organization? What would Jesus do?

Then there was his family. Of course, if he took any steps to inform the Commission, it would mean the loss of his position. His wife and daughter had always enjoyed luxury and a good place in society. If he came out against this lawlessness as a witness, it would drag him into courts. His motives would be misunderstood. The whole thing would end in his disgrace and the loss of his position.

Surely it was none of his business. He could easily get the papers back to the freight department and no one would be the wiser. Let the inquiry go on. Let the law be defied. What was it to him? He would work out his plans for bettering the conditions just before him. What more could a man do in this railroad business when there was so much going on anyway that made it impossible to live by the Christian standard? But what would Jesus do if He knew the facts? That was the question that confronted Alexander Powers as the day wore into evening.

The lights in the office had been turned on. The whirr of the machines in the big shop continued until six o'clock.

Then the whistle blew. The men dropped their tools, hurried to wash up, change their clothes and head for home. Powers said to his clerks, "I'm not going just yet. I have some extra work tonight."

At seven o'clock anyone who had looked into the superintendent's office would have seen an unusual sight. He was kneeling by his desk, his face buried in his hands.

5

When Rachel Winslow and Virginia Page separated after the meeting at the First Church on Sunday, they agreed to continue their conversation the next day. Virginia asked Rachel to come and lunch with her at noon, and Rachel accordingly rang the bell at the Page mansion about half-past eleven. Virginia herself met her, and the two were soon talking earnestly.

"The fact is," Rachel was saying, after they had been talking a few moments, "I cannot reconcile it with my judgment of what Christ would do. I cannot tell another person what to do, but I feel that I ought not to accept this offer."

"What will you do, then?" asked Virginia with great interest.

"I don't know yet. But I have decided to refuse this offer."

Rachel picked up a letter that had been lying in her lap and ran over its contents again. It was a letter offering her a place in a comic opera with a large company, traveling for the season. The salary was a very good figure, and the prospect held out by the manager of the company was flattering. He had heard Rachel sing that Sunday morning when the stranger had interrupted the service. He had been much impressed. There was money in that voice and it ought to be used in comic opera, so said the letter, and the manager wanted a reply as soon as possible.

"There's no great virtue in saying no to this offer when I have the other one," Rachel went on thoughtfully. "That's harder to decide. But I've about made up my mind. To tell the truth, Virginia, I'm completely convinced in the first case that Jesus would never use any talent like a good voice just to make money. But now take this concert offer. Here is a reputable company with which to travel. It includes an im-personator, a violinist and a male quartet. All are people of good reputation. I'm asked to go as one of the chorale and sing lead soprano. The salary—I mentioned it, didn't I?—is to be guaranteed $500 a month for the season. But I don't feel satisfied that Jesus would go. What do you think?"

"You mustn't ask me to decide for you," replied Virginia with a sad smile. "I believe Mr. Maxwell was right when he said we must each one of us decide according to the judgment we feel for ourselves to be Christlike. I am having a harder time than you are, dear, to decide what He would do."

"Are you?" Rachel asked. She rose and walked over to the window and looked out. Virginia came and stood by her. The street was crowded with life, and the two women looked at it silently for a moment. Suddenly Virginia broke out as Rachel had never heard her before.

"Rachel, what does all this contrast in conditions mean to you as you ask this question of what Jesus would do? It maddens me to think that the society in which I have been brought up, the society to which we both belong, is satisfied year after year to go on dressing and eating and having a good time, and giving and receiving entertainment, spending money on houses and luxuries and, to ease its conscience, occasionally donating a little money to charity without any personal sacrifice.

"Like you, I've been educated in one of the most expensive schools in America, launched into society as an heiress. Supposed to be in a most enviable position. I'm perfectly well. I have had numerous offers of marriage. I can travel or stay at home. I can gratify almost any want or desire, and yet . . . when I honestly try to imagine Jesus living the life I have lived and am expected to live, and doing for the rest of my life what thousands of other rich people do, I am under condemnation for being one of the most selfish, useless creatures in all the world. I have not looked out of this window for weeks without a feeling of horror toward myself as I see the humanity that passes by this house."

Virginia turned away and walked up and down the room. Rachel watched her and could not repress the rising tide of her own growing definition of discipleship. Of what Christian use was her own talent of song? Was the best she could do to sell her talent for so much a month, go on a concert company's tour, dress beautifully, enjoy the excitement of public applause and gain a reputation as a great singer? Was that what Jesus would do?

She was not morbid. She was in sound health, was conscious of her special gifts as a singer, and knew that if she went out into public life she could make money and achieve fame. It is doubtful if she overestimated her ability to accomplish all of that she was capable. And Virginia—what she had just said smote Rachel with great force because of the similar position in which the two friends found themselves.

Lunch was announced and they went out and were joined by Virginia's grandmother, Madame Florence Page, a handsome, stately woman of 65, and Virginia's brother, Rollin, a young man who spent most of his time at one of the clubs. Rollin had no ambition for anything. But he did have a growing admiration for Rachel Winslow, and whenever she dined at the Pages', if he knew of it, he always planned to be at home.

These three made up the Page family. Virginia's father had been a banker and grain speculator. Her mother had died ten years before, her father within the past year. The grandmother, a Southern woman in birth and training, had all the traditions and feeling that accompany the possession of wealth and social standing. She was a shrewd, careful businesswoman of more than average ability. To a large measure, the family property and wealth was invested under her personal care. Virginia's portion was her own without any restriction. She had been trained by her father to understand the ways of the business world, and even the grandmother had been compelled to acknowledge the girl's capacity for taking care of her own money.

Perhaps two persons could not be found anywhere less capable of understanding a girl like Virginia than Madame Page and Rollin. Rachel, who had known the family for many years, could not help thinking of what confronted Virginia in her own home when she once decided on the course which she honestly believed Jesus would take. Today at lunch, as she recalled Virginia's outbreak in the front room, she tried to picture the scene that would at some time occur between Madame Page and her granddaughter.

"I understand that you are going on the stage, Miss Winslow. We are all delighted for you," said Rollin during the conversation that had not been very animated.

Rachel reddened and felt annoyed.

"Who told you?" she asked, while Virginia, who had been very silent and reserved, suddenly roused herself and appeared ready to join in the talk.

Rollin quickly responded, "Oh, we hear a thing or two on the street. Besides, everyone saw that talent manager at church two weeks ago. He doesn't go to church to hear the preaching. In fact, I know other people who don't, either, not when there's something better to hear."

Rachel did not change color this time, but she answered quietly:

"You're mistaken. I'm not going on the stage."

"It's a great pity. You'd make a hit. Everybody is talking about your singing." Rollin seemed nonplussed.

Before Rachel could say anything, Virginia broke in.

"Whom do you mean by 'everybody'?"

"Whom? I mean all the people who hear Miss Winslow on Sunday. What other time do they hear her? It's a great pity, I say, that the general public outside of Raymond cannot hear her voice."

"Please, let us talk about something else," said Rachel a little sharply. Madame Page glanced at her and spoke with a gentle courtesy.

"My dear, Rollin never could pay an indirect compliment. He is like his father in that. But we are all curious to know something of your plans. We claim the right from old acquaintance, you know. And Virginia had already told us of your concert company offer."

"I supposed, of course, that was public property," said Virginia, smiling across the table. "I was in the *News* office day before yesterday."

"Yes, yes," replied Rachel hastily. "I understand that, Madame Page. Well, Virginia and I have been talking about it. I have decided not to accept, and that is as far as I have gone as yet."

Rachel was conscious of the fact that the conversation had, up to this point, been narrowing her hesitation concerning the company's offer. She wanted a solution that would absolutely satisfy her own judgment of Jesus's probable action. It had been the last thing in the world, however, that she had desired to have her decision made in any way so public as this. Somehow what Rollin Page had said and his manner in saying it had hastened her in the matter.

"Would you mind telling us, Rachel, your reasons for refusing the offer? It looks like a great opportunity for a young girl like you. Don't you think the general public ought to hear you? I feel like Rollin about that. A voice like yours belongs to a larger audience than Raymond and the First Church."

Rachel Winslow shrank from making her plans or her thought public. But with all her repression, there was possible in her an occasional sudden breaking out that was simply an impulsive, thoroughly truthful expressing of her most inner personal feeling. She spoke now in this way.

"I have no other reason than a conviction that Jesus Christ would do the same thing," she said, looking into Madame Page's eyes with a clear, earnest gaze.

Madame Page looked aghast and Rollin stared. Before her grandmother could say anything, Virginia spoke. The rising color on each cheek showed how she was stirred.

"Grandmother, I told you we have both promised to make that the standard of our conduct for a year. We have not been able to arrive at our decisions rapidly. The difficulty in knowing what Jesus would do has perplexed Rachel and me a good deal."

Madame Page sat up a little straighter in her chair, gathering her expensive finery about her in an authoritative way. She looked straight at Virginia before she spoke.

"Of course, I understand Mr. Maxwell's statements. They are perfectly impractical to put into practice. I felt confident at the time that those who promised would find this out after a trial and abandon the whole idea as visionary and absurd. I have nothing to say about Miss Winslow's decisions, but"—she paused and continued with a sharpness that was new to Rachel—"I hope you have no foolish notions in this matter Virginia."

"I have a great many notions," replied Virginia quietly. "Whether they are foolish or not depends upon my right understanding of what He would do. As soon as I find out, I shall act."

"Excuse me, ladies," said Rollin, rising from the table. "The conversation is getting beyond my depth."

He left the dining room and there was silence for a moment. Madame Page was angry and her anger was formidable, although checked in some measure by the presence of Rachel.

"I am older by several years than you young ladies," she said, and her hauteur seemed to Rachel to rise up like a great frozen wall between them. "What you have promised in a spirit of what I call false emotion, is impossible to perform."

"Do you mean, Grandmother, that we cannot possibly act as our Lord would, or do you mean that if we try to, we shall offend the customs and prejudices of society?" asked Virginia.

"It is not required! It is not necessary! Besides, how can you act with any—"

Madame Page paused, broke off her sentence, and then turned to Rachel.

"What will your mother say to your decision? My dear, is it not foolish? What do you expect to do with your voice anyway?"

"I don't know what Mother will say yet," Rachel answered, with a sudden shrinking from trying to give her mother's probable answer. If there was a woman in all Raymond with great ambitions for her daughter's success as a singer, Mrs. Winslow was that woman.

"Oh, you will see it in a different light after wise thought. Furthermore," continued Madame Page, rising from the table, "you will live to regret it if you do not accept the concert company's offer or something like it."

Rachel left soon after, feeling that her departure was to be followed by a very painful conversation between Virginia and her grandmother. As she afterward learned, Virginia passed through a crisis of feeling during that scene with her grandmother that hastened her final decision as to the use of her money and her social position.

6

Rachel was glad to escape and be by herself. She needed to be alone to carefully think through the plan taking form in her mind. So it was to her annoyance that before she had walked two blocks she became aware of Rollin Page walking beside her.

"Sorry to disturb your thought, Miss Winslow, but I happened to be going your way and had an idea you might not object. In fact, I've been walking beside you for a whole block and you haven't objected."

"I did not see you," said Rachel.

"I wouldn't mind that if you only thought of me once in a while," said Rollin suddenly.

Rachel was surprised. She had known Rollin as a boy and there had been a time when they had used each other's first names familiarly. Lately, however, something in Rachel's manner had put an end to that. She was used to his direct attempts at compliment and was sometimes amused by them. Today she honestly wished him anywhere else.

"Do you ever think of me, Miss Winslow?" asked Rollin after a pause.

"Oh yes, quite often!" said Rachel with a smile.

"Are you thinking of me now?"

"Yes, that is—yes, I am."

"What?"

"Do you want me to be absolutely truthful?"

"Of course."

"Then I was thinking that I wished you were not here."

Rollin bit his lip and looked gloomy.

"Now look here, Rachel. What makes you treat me so? You used to like me a little, you know."

"Did I? Of course we used to get on very well as children. But we are older now."

Rachel still spoke in the light, easy way she had used since her first awareness of his presence. She was still somewhat preoccupied with her thinking, which had been disturbed by Rollin's appearance.

They walked along in silence a little way. The avenue was full of people. Among the persons passing was Jasper Chase. He saw Rachel and Rollin and nodded as they went by. Rollin was watching Rachel closely.

"I wish I were Jasper Chase; maybe I'd stand a chance then," he said moodily.

Rachel reddened in spite of herself. She did not say anything, and quickened her pace a little. Rollin seemed determined to say something and Rachel seemed helpless to prevent him.

"You know well enough, Rachel, how I feel toward you. I could make you happy. I've loved you a good many years—"

"Why, how old do you think I am?" broke in Rachel with a nervous laugh.

"You know what I mean," went on Rollin doggedly. "And you have no right to laugh at me just because I want you to marry me."

"I'm not laughing at you. But it is useless for you to talk about it, Rollin," said Rachel after a little hesitation. "The whole thing is just impossible."

"Would—that is—do you think—if you gave me time I would—"

"No!" said Rachel. She spoke firmly. Perhaps, she thought afterwards, she had spoken harshly, although she had not meant to.

They walked on for some time without a word. They were nearing Rachel's home and she was anxious to end the scene.

As they turned off the avenue into one of the quieter streets, Rollin spoke suddenly and with more vitality than he had yet shown. There was a dignity in his voice that was new to Rachel.

"Rachel, I ask you to be my wife. Will you consider this seriously?"

"No," Rachel said decidedly.

"Will you tell me why?" He asked the question as if he had a right to a truthful answer.

"I do not love you, and I cannot."

"Why?" That was another question and Rachel was a little surprised that he should ask it.

"Because—" she hesitated for fear she might say too much in an attempt to speak the exact truth.

"Just tell me why. You can't hurt me any more than you have already."

"Well, I do not and cannot love you because you have no purpose in life. What do you ever do to make the world better? You spend your time in club life, in amusements, in travel, in luxury. What is there in such a life to attract a woman?"

"Not much, I guess," said Rollin with a little laugh. "Still, I don't know as I am any worse than the rest of the men around me. I'm not so bad as some. But I'm glad to know your reason."

He suddenly stopped, took off his hat, bowed gravely and turned his back. Rachel went on home and hurried up the stairs to her room, disturbed in many ways by the whole experience.

When she had had time to think it all over, she found herself condemned by the very judgment she had passed on Rollin Page. What purpose had *she* in life? She had been abroad and studied music with one of the famous teachers in Europe. She had come home to Raymond and had been singing in the First Church choir now for a year. She was well-paid. Up to that Sunday two weeks ago she had been quite satisfied with herself and with her position. She had shared her mother's ambition and anticipated growing triumphs in the musical world. What possible career was before her except the regular career of every singer?

She asked the question again and again and, in the light of her recent reply to Rollin, wondered if she had any very great purpose in life herself? What would Jesus do? There was a fortune in her voice. She knew it, not necessarily as a matter of personal pride or professional egotism, but simply as a fact. And she was obliged to acknowledge that until two weeks ago she had planned to use her voice to make money and win admiration and applause. Was that a higher purpose, after all, than Rollin Page lived for?

She sat in her room a long time and finally went downstairs resolved that before dinner, she would have a frank talk with her mother about the concert company's offer and the new plan which was gradually shaping in her mind. She knew her mother expected her to enter into a career as a professional singer.

Mrs. Jennifer Winslow was a large, handsome woman, fond of entertaining, ambitious for distinction in society, and devoted, according to her definition of success, to the success of her children. Her youngest boy, Lewis, two years younger than Rachel, was ready to graduate from a military academy in the summer. Meanwhile, she and Rachel lived at home together. Her husband had died several years before.

"Mother," Rachel said, coming at once to the point, as much as she dreaded the interview, "I have decided not to go out with the concert company. I have a good reason for it."

Mrs. Winslow frowned, but waited for Rachel to go on.

"You know the promise I made two weeks ago, Mother?"

"Mr. Maxwell's promise?"

"No, mine. Remember what it was, Mother?"

"I suppose I do. Of course, all the church members mean to imitate Christ and follow Him as far as is consistent with our present-day surroundings. But what has that to do with your decision in the matter of the concert company?"

"It has everything to do with it. After asking, 'What would Jesus do?' and praying for wisdom, I have been obliged to say that I do not believe He would, in my case, make that use of my voice."

"Why? Is there anything wrong about such a career?"

"No, I don't know that I can say there is."

"Do you presume to sit in judgment on other people who go out to sing in this way? Do you presume to say that they are doing what Christ would not do?"

"Mother, I wish you to understand me. I judge no one else. I condemn no other professional singers. I simply decide my own course. As I look at it, I have a conviction that Jesus would do something else."

"What else?" Mrs. Winslow had not yet lost her temper. She did not understand the situation, nor Rachel in the midst of it, but she was anxious that her daughter's course should be as distinguished as her natural gifts promised. And she felt confident that, when the present unusual religious excitement in the First Church had passed away, Rachel would go on with her professional life according to the wishes of the family.

"What else can I do? Something that will serve mankind where it most needs the service of song. Mother, I have made up my mind to use my voice in some way so as to satisfy my own soul that I am doing something better than pleasing fashionable audiences, or making money, or even gratifying my own love of singing. I am going to do something that will satisfy me when I ask, 'What would Jesus do?' I am not satisfied, and cannot be, when I think of myself as becoming a concert artist."

Rachel spoke with a vigor and earnestness that surprised her mother, but Mrs. Winslow was angry now. And she never tried to conceal her feelings.

"It is simply absurd! Rachel, you are a fanatic. What can you do?"

"I shall continue to sing for the time being in the church. I am pledged to sing there through the spring. During the week I am going to sing at the White Cross meetings down in the Rectangle."

"What! Rachel Winslow! Do you know what you are saying? Do you know what sort of people are down there?"

Rachel almost quailed before her mother. For a moment she was silent. Then she spoke firmly:

"I know very well. That is the reason I am going. Mr. and Mrs. Gray have been working there several weeks. I learned only this morning that they want singers from the churches to help them in their meetings. They use a tent. It is in a part of the city where Christian work is most needed. I shall offer them my help. Mother, don't you see?" Rachel cried out with her first passionate utterance. "I want to do something worthwhile. What have we done all our lives for the suffering side of Raymond? How much have we denied ourselves or given of our personal ease and pleasure to bless the place we live or imitate the life of the Savior of the world? Are we always to go on doing as society selfishly dictates, moving on its narrow little round of pleasures and entertainments and never knowing the pain of things that cost?"

"Are you preaching to me?" asked Mrs. Winslow slowly.

"No, I am preaching to myself," Rachel replied gently.

When she returned to her own room, she felt that, so far as her mother was concerned, she could expect no sympathy or understanding. She knelt. It was safe to say that within the two weeks since Henry Maxwell's congregation had faced that shabby figure with the faded hat, more members of his parish had been driven to their knees in prayer than during all the previous years of his pastorate.

Rachel arose and her face was wet with tears. She sat thoughtfully a little while and then stood and walked over to her bedroom window. Later at dinner, she told her mother that she and Virginia were going down to the Rectangle that evening to see Mr. and Mrs. John Gray, the evangelists.

"Dr. West is going with us. The doctor is a friend of the Grays, and attended some of the meetings during the winter."

Mrs. Winslow did not say anything. Her manner showed her complete disapproval.

The Rectangle was a barren dirt field used in the summer by circus companies and wandering showmen. It was shut in by rows of saloons, gambling halls and cheap boardinghouses and was bordered by railroad yards and packing houses. The slum and tenement districts of Raymond formed a wider congested area all about the Rectangle.

The First Church of Raymond had never really touched the Rectangle problem. It was too dirty, too sinful a place for close contact. There had been an attempt to cleanse this sore spot by sending down an occasional committee of singers, or Sunday school teachers, or Gospel visitors from various churches. But the First Church of Raymond as an institution had never done anything to make the Rectangle any less a stronghold of the devil as the years went by.

Into this heart of the sin of Raymond, a traveling evangelist and his brave little wife had pitched a good-sized tent and begun meetings. It was now the spring of the year and the evenings were beginning to be pleasant. The evangelists had asked for the help of Christian people and had received more than the usual amount of encouragement. But they felt a need of more and better music. During the meetings on the Sunday just past, the assistant at the organ had been taken ill. The volunteers from the city were few and the voices of ordinary quality.

"There will be a small meeting tonight, John," said his wife, as they entered the tent a little after seven o'clock and began to arrange the chairs.

"Yes, I fear so." Mr. Gray was a small, energetic man with a pleasant voice and the courage of a lion tamer. He had already made friends in the neighborhood, and one of his converts, a heavy-faced man who had just come in, began to help in the arranging of the seats.

It was after eight o'clock when Alexander Powers opened the door of his office and started for home. He was going to take a streetcar at the corner of the Rectangle. But he was stopped by a voice coming from the tent, a voice he had heard many times before.

It was the voice of Rachel Winslow. It interrupted his mental groping over a problem that had sent him to his knees for an answer. He had not yet reached a conclusion. He was tortured with uncertainty. His whole previous course of action as a railroad man was the poorest possible preparation for anything sacrificial.

What was she singing? How did Rachel Winslow happen to be down here? Several nearby windows went up. Some men quarreling in a saloon stopped and listened. Other figures were walking in the direction of the Rectangle and the tent.

Rachel Winslow had never sung like that in the First Church. Again Alexander Powers, Superintendent of the Machine Shops, paused and listened.

> Where He leads me I will follow,
> Where He leads me I will follow,
> Where He leads me I will follow,
> I'll go with Him, with Him,
> All the way.

The brutal, coarse, impure life around the Rectangle stirred itself as the song, as pure as the surroundings were vile, floated out into the night air. Someone stumbling hastily by Alexander Powers said in answer to a question:

"The Tent's beginning to run over tonight. That's what they call real music, eh?"

The superintendent turned toward the tent. Then he stopped. After a minute of indecision he went on to the corner and took the streetcar home. But before he was out of the sound of Rachel's voice, he knew that he had settled for himself the question of what Jesus would do.

7

Henry Maxwell paced his study back and forth. It was Wednesday and he had started to think out the subject of his evening service.

Through one of his study windows he could see the tall chimneys of the railroad machine shop. The top of the evangelist's tent barely showed over the buildings around the Rectangle.

He looked out of his window every time he turned in his walk. After a while he sat down at his desk and drew a large piece of paper toward him.

After thinking several moments he wrote in large letters the following:

A Number of Things That Jesus Would Probably Do in This Parish

1. Live in a simple, plain manner, without needless luxury on the one hand or undue asceticism on the other.
2. Preach fearlessly to the hypocrites in the church no matter what their social importance or wealth.

3. Show in some practical form, sympathy and love for the common people as well as for the well-to-do, educated, refined people who make up the majority of the parish.

4. Identify Himself with the great causes of humanity in some personal way that would call for self-denial and sacrifice.

5. Preach against the liquor interests in Raymond.

6. Become known as a friend and companion of the people in the Rectangle.

7. Give up the summer trip to Europe this year, using the money for something more worthwhile.

He was conscious, with a humility that was once a stranger to him, that his outline of Jesus's probable action was undoubtedly lacking in depth and power, but he was seeking carefully for concrete shapes into which he might cast his thought of Jesus's conduct. Nearly every point he had put down meant, for him, a complete overturning of the custom and habit of years in the ministry. In spite of that, he still searched deeper for sources of the Christlike spirit. He did not attempt to write any more but sat at his desk absorbed in his effort to catch more and more of the Spirit of Jesus in his own life. He had forgotten the particular subject for his prayer meeting with which he had begun his morning study.

He was so absorbed in his thoughts that he did not hear the bell ring and he was roused by his wife, who announced a caller, Mr. John Gray.

Maxwell stepped to the head of the stairs and asked Mr. Gray to come up.

The evangelist did so and quickly stated the reason for his call.

"I want your help, Mr. Maxwell. You may have heard what a wonderful meeting we had Monday night and last night. Miss Winslow has done more with her voice than I could do in preaching, and the tent won't hold the people."

"So I've heard. I'm not surprised that the people are attracted."

"It has been a wonderful revelation to us, and a most encouraging event in our work. But I came to ask if you would come down tonight and preach. I am suffering from a severe cold. I do not dare to trust my voice tonight. I know it is asking a good deal from such a busy man, but if you can't come, say so frankly, and I'll try somewhere else."

"I'm sorry, but it's my regular prayer-meeting night," began Henry Maxwell. Then he flushed and added, "I shall be able to arrange it in some way so as to come down. You can count on me."

The evangelist thanked him earnestly and rose to go.

"Won't you stay a minute, Mr. Gray, and let us have a prayer together?"

So the two men knelt in the study. Henry Maxwell prayed like a child. The evangelist was moved to tears as he listened. There was something almost pitiful in the way this man who had lived his ministerial life on such a narrow basis now begged for wisdom and strength to speak a message to the people in the Rectangle.

The visitor rose and held out his hand.

"God bless you, Mr. Maxwell. I'm sure the Holy Spirit will give you power tonight."

Henry Maxwell made no answer. He did not even trust himself to say that he hoped so. But he thought of his promise, and it brought him a certain peace that was refreshing to his heart and mind alike.

So that is how it came about that when members of the First Church came into the lecture room that evening they were met with a surprise.

Mr. Maxwell came at once to the point.

"I feel that I am called to go down to the Rectangle tonight, and I will leave it with you to say whether you will go on with the meeting here. I think perhaps the best plan would be for a few volunteers to go down to the Rectangle with me, prepared to help in the after-meeting, if necessary, and the rest to remain here and pray that the Spirit's power may go with us."

So half-a-dozen of the men went with the pastor and the rest of the people stayed in the lecture room. Maxwell could not escape the thought that probably in his entire church membership there might not be found a score of disciples who were capable of doing work that would successfully lead needy, sinful men into the knowledge of Christ. The thought did not linger in his mind to vex him as he went his way, but it was simply a part of his whole new conception of the meaning of Christian discipleship.

When he and his little company of volunteers reached the Rectangle, the tent was already crowded. They had difficulty in getting to the platform. Rachel was there with Virginia and Jasper Chase, who had come with them instead of the doctor this particular night.

When the meeting began with a song in which Rachel sang the solo and the people were asked to join in the chorus, not a foot of standing room was left in the tent. The night was mild, the sides of the tent were up and a great border of faces stretched around, looking in and forming part of the audience.

After the singing and a prayer by one of the city's pastors who was present, evangelist John Gray stated the reason for his inability to speak, and with simplicity turned the service over to "Brother Maxwell of the First Church."

"Who's dat bloke?" asked a hoarse voice near the outside of the tent.

"De Fust Church parson? We've got all da highbrows here tonight."

"Did you say Fust Church? I know him. My landlord has got a front pew up there," said another voice, and there was a laugh, for the speaker was a saloon-keeper.

"Trow out de lifeline, 'cross de dark wave" began a drunken man nearby, singing in such an unconscious imitation of a traveling singer's nasal tone that roars of laughter and gruff approval rose around him. The people in the tent turned in the direction of the disturbance. There were shouts of "Throw the disturbers out!" . . . "Give the Fust Church a chance!" . . . "Song! Song! Give us another song!"

As Henry Maxwell stood up, a wave of actual terror flooded over him. This was not like preaching to the well-dressed, respectable, good-mannered people in his parish. He began to speak, but the noise and confusion increased. The evangelist went down among the people, but did not seem able to quiet them. Maxwell raised his arm and his voice. The crowd in the tent began to pay some attention, but the noise on the outside increased. In a few minutes the audience was beyond his control. He turned to Rachel with a sad smile.

"Sing something, Miss Winslow. They will listen to you," he said, and then sat down and covered his face with his hands.

It was Rachel's opportunity and she was fully equal to it. Virginia was at the organ, and Rachel asked her to play a few notes of the hymn:

> Savior, I follow on,
> Guided by Thee
> Seeing not yet the hand
> That leadeth me;
> Hushed be my heart and still,
> Fear I no farther ill,
> Only to meet Thy will,
> My will shall be.

Rachel had not sung the first line before the people in the tent were all turned toward her, hushed and reverent. Before she had finished the verse, the Rectangle was subdued and tamed. It lay like some wild beast at her feet and she sang it into harmlessness. What a contrast between the perfumed, critical audiences in concert halls and this dirty, drunken, impure, besotted mass of humanity, which trembled and wept and grew strangely, sadly thoughtful under the divine singing of this beautiful young woman.

Mr. Maxwell, as he raised his head and saw the transformed mob, had a glimpse of what Jesus could do with a voice like Rachel Winslow's. Jasper Chase sat with his eyes on the singer, and his greatest longing as an ambitious author was swallowed up in the thought of what Rachel Winslow's love might sometime mean to him. And over in the shadow, outside, stood the last person anyone might have expected to see at a gospel tent service—Rollin Page.

Jostled on every side by rough men and women who stared at his fine clothes, Rollin seemed indifferent to his surroundings and at the same time evidently swayed by the power that Rachel possessed. He had just come over from the club. Neither Rachel nor Virginia saw him that night.

The song was over. Maxwell rose again. This time he felt calmer. What would Jesus do? How would He speak to these people? Who were these people? They were immortal souls. What was Christianity? A calling of sinners, not the righteous, to repentance. And in that certainty he spoke of the love Jesus had for them and what a rich life He promised for those who became His followers.

Never before had Henry Maxwell felt such a "compassion for the multitude." What had they been to him during his ten years in the First Church? Only a vague, dangerous, dirty, troublesome factor in society. Outside of the church and of his reach, it was an element of humanity that caused him an occasional unpleasant twinge of conscience—the populace of Raymond that was talked about at association meetings as the "masses." Tonight, as he faced the "masses," he asked himself whether, after all, this was not the type of people Jesus faced, and he felt a genuine emotion of love for them.

When the meeting closed, no one stayed for the after-meeting. The people rapidly melted away from the tent, and the saloons, which had been experiencing a dull season while the meetings progressed, again drove a thriving trade. The Rectangle, as if to make up for lost time, started in with vigor on its usual night of debauchery. Maxwell and his little party, including Virginia, Rachel, and Jasper Chase, walked down past the row of tenements until they reached the corner where the streetcars passed.

"This is a terrible spot," said the minister, as they stood waiting for their car. "I never realized that Raymond had such a festering sore."

"Do you think anyone can do anything about it?" asked Jasper Chase, who had been storing up impressions and descriptions for his new manuscript.

"I have thought lately as never before of what Christian people might do. One thing—why couldn't the Christian pastors and church members of Raymond move as one man against the liquor traffic? What would Jesus do? Would He keep silent? Would he vote to license these causes of crime and death?"

He was talking to himself more than to the others. He remembered that he had always voted in favor of liquor licenses, and so had nearly all of his church members. What would Jesus do? Would the Master preach and act against the saloon, if He lived today?

The next morning he went up into his study with that question only partly answered. He thought of it all day. He was still thinking of it, and reaching certain real conclusions when the *Evening News* came. His wife brought it up and sat down a few minutes while he read to her.

The *Evening News* was at present the most sensational news in Raymond. That is to say, it was being edited in such an unusual fashion that its subscribers were in a state of constant bewilderment.

First, they had noticed the absence of the prize fight, and gradually it began to dawn upon them that the *News* no longer printed accounts of crime with detailed descriptions of, or scandals in private lives. Then they noticed that the advertisements of liquor and tobacco were dropped, together with certain others of a questionable character. The discontinuance of the Sunday paper caused the greatest comment of all. A number of readers canceled subscriptions. Others were annoyed with the changes, but intrigued enough to keep reading it.

The editorials had become unpredictable but were always attention-grabbing, like this one:

The Moral Side of Political Questions

The editor of the *News* has always advocated the principles of the political party at present in power and has, therefore, discussed all political questions from a standpoint of expediency, or of belief in the party, as opposed to other political organizations. Hereafter, the editor will present and discuss all political questions from the standpoint of right and wrong.

In other words the first question in this office about any political question will not be, Is it in the interest of our party, or, Is it according to the principles laid down by our party in its platform? But the question first asked will be, Is this measure in accordance with the spirit and teachings of Jesus, as the author of the greatest standard of life known to men? From now on, the moral side of every political question will be considered its most important side. The stand we will take is that nations as well as individuals are under the same law, to do all things to the glory of God, as the first rule of action.

The same principle will be observed in this office toward candidates for places of responsibility and trust in the Republic. Regardless of party politics, the editor of the *News* will do all in his power to bring the best men into power, and will not knowingly help to support for office any candidate who is unworthy, no matter how much he may be endorsed by the party. The first question asked about the man and about the measure will be, Is he the right man for the job? Is he a good man with ability? Is the measure right?

Hundreds of men in Raymond read the editorial and rubbed their eyes in amazement. A good many of them had promptly written to the *News* telling the editor to cancel their subscriptions. Others wrote to express their support and approval. At the end of the week, however, Edward Norman calculated that he was losing a lot more subscribers than he was gaining. He faced the conditions calmly, although Clark, the managing editor, grimly anticipated ultimate bankruptcy.

This night, as Maxwell read items from the *News* to his wife, he could see in almost every column evidence of Norman's conscientious obedience to his promise. There was an absence of slangy, sensational scare-heads. The reading matter under the headlines was in perfect keeping with them. He noticed in two columns that the reporters' names appeared, signed at the bottom. And there was a distinct advance in the dignity and style of their contributions.

"Norman is now having his reporters sign their work," the pastor said. "He has talked with me about that. It is a good thing. It fixes responsibility for an item where it belongs and raises the standard of reporting. A good thing all around, for the public and the writers."

Maxwell suddenly rattled the paper with excitement. "Listen to this, Mary," he said with trembling lips:

Alexander Powers, Superintendent of the L. and T.R.R. in this city, has handed in his resignation to the road and given as his reason the fact that proof had fallen into his hands that his company had violated the interstate commerce law, and also the state law, which was recently passed to prevent and punish railroad pooling for the benefit of certain favored shippers. Mr. Powers stated in his resignation that he could no longer withhold the information he possessed against the railroad. He will be a witness against it. He has placed his evidence in the hands of the Commission, which must now study the evidence and take whatever action is needed.

The *News* wishes to express itself on this action of Mr. Powers. In the first place, he has nothing to gain by it. He has lost a very good position, voluntarily, when he could have retained it by keeping silent. In the second place, we believe his action ought to receive the approval of all thoughtful, honest citizens, who believe in seeing our laws obeyed and lawbreakers brought to justice. In a case like this, evidence against a railroad company is almost impossible to obtain. It is the general belief that the officers of the railroad are often in possession of incriminating facts, but do not consider it to be their duty to inform the authorities that the law is being defied. The result of this evasion of responsibility on the part of railroad officials is demoralizing to young employees.

The editor of the *News* recalls the statement made recently by a prominent railroad official in this city that nearly every clerk in a certain department knew that large sums of money were being made by shrewd violations of the interstate commerce law. They were inclined to admire the shrewdness with which the law was being broken, and declared that they would all do the same thing if they became high officials in the railroad.

It is hardly necessary to say that such a condition of business is destructive to good standards of conduct. No young man can live in such an atmosphere of unpunished dishonesty and not have it influence his character.

In our judgment, Mr. Powers did the only thing that a committed Christian man can do. He has rendered brave and useful service to the state and general public. There are times when the individual must act for the people in ways that will mean sacrifice and loss to himself of the gravest character. Mr. Powers will be misunderstood and misrepresented, but there is no question that his course will be approved by every citizen who wishes to see the powerful corporations, as well as the weakest individual, subject to the same law. It now remains for the Commission to act upon the evidence, which we understand is overwhelming proof of the lawlessness of the L. and T. Let the law be enforced, no matter who the persons may be who are guilty.

8

Henry Maxwell finished reading and dropped the paper.

"I must go and see Powers. This is the result of his promise."

He rose, and as he was going out his wife said, "Do you think, Henry, that Jesus would have done that?"

Maxwell paused a moment. Then thoughtfully replied "Yes, I think He would. At any rate, Powers has decided so, and each one of us who made the promise understands that he is not deciding Jesus's conduct for anyone but himself."

"How about his family? How will Mrs. Powers and Celia be likely to take it?"

"Very hard, I have no doubt. That will be Powers' cross in this matter. They will not understand his motive."

Maxwell went out and walked over to the next block where the Powers lived. To his relief, Powers himself came to the door.

The two men shook hands silently. They instantly understood each other, without words. There had never before been such a bond of union between the minister and his parishioner.

"What are you going to do?" Henry Maxwell asked after they had talked over the facts in the case.

"You mean another position? I have no plans yet. I can go back to my old work as a telegraph operator. My family will not suffer except in a social way."

Powers spoke calmly but sadly. Henry Maxwell did not need to ask him how his wife and daughter felt. He knew well enough that the former superintendent had suffered most deeply at that point.

"There is one matter I wish you would see to," said Powers after a while, "and that concerns the project I started for the workmen. So far as I know, the company will not object to that going on. Though lawless acts may be committed by the official management itself, they still want to employ men who are temperate, honest, and Christian. So I have no doubt that my successor, Arnold Stone, will have the same courtesy shown him in the use of the room. You made a favorable impression on the men. Would you go down there as often as you can? And please get Arnold Stone interested in providing something for the furnishings and expense of the coffeemaker and reading tables. Will you do it?"

"Yes," replied Henry Maxwell. Before parting, Maxwell and Powers prayed together.

The pastor of the First Church went home deeply stirred by the events of the week. Gradually the truth was growing on him that the pledge to do as Jesus would was working out a revolution in his parish and throughout the city. Every day added to the serious results of obedience to that pledge. Maxwell did not pretend to see the end. He was, in fact, only now at the very beginning of events that were destined to change the history of hundreds of families, not only in Raymond but throughout the entire country.

As he thought of Edward Norman and Rachel and Mr. Powers, and of the results that had already come from their actions, he could not help feeling an intense interest in the probable effect, if all those persons in First Church who had made the pledge faithfully kept it. Would they all keep it, or would some of them turn back when the cross became too heavy?

He was asking this question the next morning as he sat in his study, when the president of the Endeavor Society called to see him.

"I suppose I ought not to trouble you with my case," said young Fred Morris, coming at once to the purpose of his errand. "But I thought, Mr. Maxwell, that you might advise me a little."

"I'm glad you came. Go on, Fred." Henry Maxwell had known the young man ever since he first came to the pastorate, and loved and honored him for his consistent, faithful service in the church.

"Well, the fact is, I'm out of a job. You know I've been doing reporting for the *Morning Sentinel* since I graduated last year. Well, last Saturday my boss asked me to take Sunday morning for digging up the details of that train robbery at the Junction, and write the thing up for the extra edition that comes out Monday morning. I refused to work on Sunday and he gave me my dismissal. The boss was in a bad temper, or I think perhaps he would not have done it. He has always treated me well before. Now, do you think Jesus would have done as I did? I asked because the other fellows say I was a fool not to do the work. I want to feel that a Christian acts from motives that may seem strange to others sometimes, but not foolish. What do you think?"

I think you kept your promise, Fred. I cannot believe Jesus would do newspaper work on Sunday as you were asked to do it."

"Thank you, Mr. Maxwell. I felt a little troubled over it, but the longer I think about it the better I feel."

As young Morris rose to leave, his pastor laid a loving hand on his shoulder.

"Where are you going to go, Fred?"

"I don't know yet. I have thought some of going to Chicago, or some other large city."

"Why don't you try the *News*?"

"They are fully staffed, or so I've heard."

Maxwell pondered a moment. "Come down to the *News* office with me and let's see Edward Norman."

So a few minutes later, Edward Norman received into his office the minister and young Morris. Maxwell briefly stated the reason for their visit.

"I can give you a place on the *News*," said Norman with a smile. "I want reporters who won't work on Sundays. And what is more, I am making plans for a special kind of reporting which I believe you can help me develop."

When Henry Maxwell began the nine-block walk back to his home he was feeling that deep satisfaction which comes from being God's servant. Starting to pass Milton Wright's main store, he hesitated, then on impulse walked inside.

The balding, middle-aged merchant greeted him warmly. "Come to my office where we can talk," he urged.

Once they were seated in Wright's comfortable private office, the businessman leaned forward intently. "Since making that commitment to follow Jesus, I have been compelled to change the entire operation of my company. During the last twenty years I have done many things that I know Jesus would not have done. Now I'm suddenly aware of many things that He *would* do in this business."

"What was the first change you made?" Henry Maxwell suddenly felt that his sermon preparation could wait.

"The first change I had to make was in my thinking about my employees. I came down here Monday morning after that Sunday and asked myself, What would Jesus do in His relationship to these clerks, bookkeepers, office boys, salesmen? Would He try to establish some sort of personal relationship to them different from that which I have sustained all these years? I soon answered the question with a yes. Then came the question, What was I to do? I did not see how I could answer it to my satisfaction without getting all of my employees together and having a talk with them. So we had a meeting out in the warehouse Tuesday night.

"A good many things came out of that meeting. I can't tell you all. I tried to talk with the men as I imagined Jesus might. It was hard work, for I have not been in the habit of it, and must have made mistakes. But I can hardly describe to you, Pastor, the effect of that meeting on some of the men. Before it closed, I saw more than a dozen of them had tears on their faces. I kept asking, what would Jesus do? And the more I asked it, the farther along I was pushed into personal dealings with the men who have worked for me all these years. Right now I am in the midst of reconstructing the entire business, insofar as all our personnel operations are concerned. I have not yet reached definite conclusions in regard to all the details. I am not sufficiently knowledgeable of Jesus's methods. But let me show you something."

Wright reached up into one of his desk drawers, took out a paper and handed it to his pastor.

"I have sketched out what seems to me a plan such as Jesus might go by in a business like mine. I want you to tell me what you think of it."

What Jesus Would Probably Do in Milton Wright's Place as a Businessman

1. He would engage in the business first of all for the purpose of glorifying God, and not for the primary purpose of making money.
2. All profit achieved He would not regard as His own, but as trust funds to be used for the good of humanity.
3. His relationships with all employees would be loving and helpful. He would think of them in the light of souls to be saved. This thought would always be of greater importance than making money.
4. He would never do a single dishonest or questionable act or try in any way to take advantage of anyone else.
5. The principle of unselfishness and helpfulness in the business would direct all its details.

6. Upon these principles He would shape the entire plan of His relationships to His employees, to His customers, and to the general business world with which He was connected.

Henry Maxwell read this over slowly. It reminded him of his own attempts the day before to put into a concrete form his ideas of Jesus's probable action. He was very thoughtful as he looked up and met Wright's eager gaze.

"Do you believe you can continue to make your business pay operating on those principles?"

"I do. Intelligent unselfishness ought to be wiser than intelligent selfishness, don't you think? If my employees begin to have a personal share in the profits of the business, and, more than that, feel a personal love for themselves on the part of the management, won't the result be more care, less waste, more diligence, more faithfulness?"

"Yes, I would certainly think so. Yet a good many other businessmen wouldn't agree, would they? I mean as a general rule. How about your relations to the people you deal with in the world who will consider your plan completely unbusinesslike?"

"That complicates my action, of course."

"Does your plan contemplate what is coming to be known as management-employee cooperation?"

"Yes, it does, so far as I have gone. I am absolutely convinced that Jesus, in my place, would be absolutely unselfish. He would love all these men in His employ. He would consider the main purpose of all business to be a mutual helpfulness, and would conduct it all so that God's Kingdom would be the first object sought."

When Maxwell finally left he was profoundly impressed with the revolution that was being wrought already in this business. There was no mistaking the fact that Milton Wright's new relationship to his employees was beginning, even after less than two weeks, to transform the atmosphere of the store. This was apparent even in the faces of the clerks.

"If he keeps on, he will be one of the most influential preachers in Raymond," said Henry Maxwell to himself as he reached his study. He wondered if Milton Wright would continue his plan if he began to lose money, as was possible. He prayed that the Holy Spirit, who had shown Himself with growing power in the company of the First Church disciples, would abide long with them all. And with that prayer on his lips and in his heart, he began the preparation of his sermon for the coming Sunday.

Saturday night at the Rectangle there occurred some of the most remarkable scenes that Mr. Gray and his wife had ever witnessed. The meetings had intensified with each night of Rachel's singing. It cannot be said that, up to that Saturday night, there was any appreciable decrease in the heavy drinking, coarse language, and immorality throughout the area. The Rectangle had too much local pride in being tough. But in spite of itself, there was a gradual yielding to a new power it had never quite before experienced.

Mr. Gray had recovered his voice, so that by Saturday he was able to speak. The fact that he was obliged to use his voice carefully made it necessary for the people to be very quiet if they wanted to hear. Gradually they had come to understand, during these many weeks, that out of a perfectly unselfish love for them, this dedicated man was giving his time and strength to bring them knowledge of a Savior. Tonight the crowd was as quiet as Henry Maxwell's decorous audience ever was. The fringe around the tent was deeper, and the saloons were practically empty. The evangelist felt that one of the great prayers of his life was going to be answered.

And Rachel—her singing seemed to Virginia Page and Jasper Chase to be more eloquent than ever. They had come together again tonight, this time with Dr. West, who had spent all his spare time that week in the Rectangle with some charity cases. Virginia was at the organ, Jasper sat on a front seat. After the message the Rectangle seemed to sway as one man toward the platform when Rachel began to sing:

> Just as I am, without one plea,
> But that Thy blood was shed for me,
> And that Thou bidst me come to Thee,
> O Lamb of God, I come, I come.

Gray hardly said a word. He stretched out his hand with a gesture of invitation. And down the two aisles of the tent, a line of men and women moved toward the front. One woman out of the street was near the organ. Virginia caught the look on her face, and for the first time in the life of this rich girl, the thought of what Jesus was to that sinful woman came with a suddenness and power that was like new birth. Virginia left the organ, went to her, looked into the woman's face and caught both her hands in her own. Clinging to Virginia, the woman fell on her knees sobbing, her head resting upon the back of the rude bench in front of her. Virginia, after a moment's hesitation, knelt beside her and the two heads were bowed close together.

As the people crowded in a double row all about the platform, most of them kneeling and crying, a man in evening dress pushed through the seats and came and knelt with the others. By his side was the same drunken man who had disturbed the meeting the night Maxwell had spoken. The young man was kneeling within a few feet of Rachel Winslow, who was still singing softly. She turned for a moment and looked in his direction and was amazed to see the face of Rollin Page. For a moment her voice faltered. Then she went on:

> Just as I am, Thou wilt receive,
> Wilt welcome, pardon, cleanse, relieve;
> Because Thy promise I believe,
> O Lamb of God, I come, I come.

9

It was nearly midnight before the service at the Rectangle closed. Mr. Gray stayed up long into Sunday morning, praying and talking to many of the converts who, in the great emotion of their new life, clung to the evangelist with a personal helplessness as if they were depending upon him to save them from physical death. Among these was Rollin Page.

Sometime after midnight Jasper Chase sat in his room staring at the papers on his desk and going over the past hour with painful persistence. While walking Rachel home, he had told her that he loved her. Rachel had not given her love in return.

He had yielded to his feelings because he had felt so certain that Rachel would respond to his love. What he gone wrong?

Never before had her beauty and her vitality influenced him as it had tonight. While she was singing he saw and heard no one else. The tent swarmed with a confused crowd of faces, and he knew he was sitting there hemmed in by a mob of people; but he saw only Rachel. He felt powerless to avoid speaking of his love to her.

Now that he had spoken, he felt that he had misjudged either Rachel or the time. He had been sure that she cared something for him. It was no secret between them that the heroine of Jasper's first novel had been his own portrait of Rachel. The hero in the story was himself, and they had loved each other in the book. No one else knew. The names and characters had been drawn with a subtle skill that revealed to Rachel the fact of his love for her. She had not been offended then, and that was nearly a year ago.

Tonight he recalled the scene between them with every inflection and movement etched in his memory. He even recalled the fact that he began to speak just at that point on the avenue where, a few days before, he had met Rachel walking with Rollin Page. He had wondered at the time what Rollin was saying.

"Rachel," Jasper had begun, "I never knew until tonight how much I love you. Why should I try to conceal it any longer? You know I love you as my life."

The first intimation he had of a repulse was the very calmness of Rachel's reaction. She had allowed him to speak and had neither turned her face toward him nor away from him. She had looked straight on, and her voice was sad but firm and quiet when she spoke.

"Why do you speak to me now? I cannot bear it—after what we have seen tonight."

"Why—what—?" he had stammered, and then was silent. Rachel withdrew her arm from his, but still walked near him. Then he had cried out, with the anguish of one who begins to see a great loss facing him where he had expected a great joy.

"Rachel! Do you not love me?"

She had walked silently for a few steps after that. They had passed a street lamp. Her face was pale and beautiful. He had made a movement to grab her arm. And she had moved a little apart from him.

"No," she had replied. "There was a time—but that is past—you should not have spoken to me now."

He had seen in these words his answer. He was extremely sensitive. Nothing short of a joyous response to his own love would ever have satisfied him. He could not think of pleading with her.

"Sometime—when I am more worthy?" he had asked in a low voice; but she did not seem to hear, and they had parted at her home. He recalled vividly the fact that no goodnight had been said.

Now as he went over the brief but significant scene, he lashed himself for his foolish haste. He had not reckoned on Rachel's tense, passionate absorption of all her feeling in the scenes at the tent, which were so new in her mind. But he did not know her well enough, even yet, to understand the meaning of her refusal. When the clock in the First Church struck one, he was still sitting at his desk, staring at the top page of the manuscript of his unfinished novel.

Rachel Winslow went up to her room and faced her evening's experience with conflicting emotions. Had she ever loved Jasper Chase? Yes. No. One moment she felt that her life's happiness was at stake over the result of her action. Another, she had a strange feeling of relief that she had spoken as she had.

There was one great overmastering feeling in her—the response of the people in the tent to her singing. The swift, powerful, awesome presence of the Holy Spirit had affected her as never in all her life before. The moment Jasper had spoken her name, and she realized that he was telling her of his love, she felt a sudden revulsion for him. Had he no respect for the supernatural events they had just witnessed? The thought that all the time she was singing with the complete passion of her soul to touch the conscience of that tent, Jasper Chase had been unmoved by it except to love her for herself, made his feeling for her seem irreverent. She could not tell why she felt as she did, only she knew that if he had not told her tonight, she would still have felt the same toward him as she always had. What was that feeling? What had he been to her?

She went to her bookcase and took out the novel Jasper had given her, then turned to certain passages she had read often, and which she knew Jasper had written for her. She read them again. Somehow they no longer touched her strongly. She closed the book and let it lie on the table.

Her thoughts turned to the sights she had witnessed in the tent. Those faces! Men and women, touched for the first time with the Spirit's glory! What a wonderful experience life could be. The complete regeneration revealed in the sight of drunken, debauched humans kneeling down to give themselves to a life of purity and Christlikeness—here was surely a witness to the divine power in the world! And the face of Rollin Page by the side of that miserable creature out of the gutter—she could recall as if she now saw it.

And Virginia crying, with her arms around her brother. And Mr. Gray kneeling close by. And the forlorn woman Virginia had taken into her heart! All these pictures drawn by the Holy Spirit, in the human tragedies brought to a climax there in the most abandoned spot in all Raymond, stood out in Rachel's memory now—a memory so recent that her room seemed for the time being to contain all the actors and their movements.

"No! No!" she had said aloud. "He had no right to speak after all that! He should have respected the place where our thoughts should have been! I am sure I do not love him. Not enough to give him my life!"

The people of Raymond awoke Sunday morning to a growing knowledge of events that stirred the community to its depths. Alexander Powers' action in the matter of the railroad frauds had created a sensation, not only in Raymond but throughout the country. Edward Norman's daily changes of policy in the conduct of his paper had startled the community and caused more comment than any recent political event. Rachel Winslow's singing at the Rectangle meetings had made a stir in society and excited the wonder of all her friends. Virginia's conduct, her presence every night with Rachel, her absence from all the usual circle of her wealthy, fashionable acquaintances, had furnished a great deal of material for gossip and question. In addition to the events centering about these persons who were so well known, there had been strange happenings all through the city, in homes, businesses, and social circles.

Nearly one hundred people in Henry Maxwell's church had made the pledge to take certain steps after asking, "What would Jesus do?" In many cases the result had been unheard-of actions. As a climax to the week's events had come the remarkable demonstration at the Rectangle, including conversions of nearly fifty of the worst characters in that neighborhood, together with the transformation of Rollin Page, the well-known clubman.

It is no wonder that members of the First Church of Raymond came to the Sunday morning service in a mood of keen expectancy.

Perhaps nothing had astonished the people more than the great change that had come over the minister since he had proposed to them the imitation of Jesus in conduct. The self-satisfied, contented attitude of the refined person in the pulpit had been displaced by a manner that was sometimes hesitant, much less assured, and yet appealing and winsome.

The sermon had become a message. It was no longer delivered. It was brought to them with a love, an earnestness, a passion, a desire, a humility that poured its enthusiasm into the truth and made the speaker no more prominent than he had to be as the living voice of God. His prayers were unlike any the people had ever heard before. They were often broken; even once or twice they had been actually ungrammatical in a phrase or two. When had Henry Maxwell so far forgotten himself in a prayer as to make a mistake of that sort?

He knew that he had often taken as much pride in the diction and delivery of his prayers as of his sermons. Was it possible he now so abhorred the elegant refinement of a formal public petition that he purposely chose to rebuke himself for his previous precise manner of prayer? It is more likely that he had no thought of all that. His great longing to voice the needs and wants of his people made him unmindful of an occasional mistake. It is certain that he had never prayed so effectively as he did now.

There are times when a sermon has a value and power due to conditions in the audience rather than to anything new or startling or eloquent in the words said or the arguments presented. Such conditions faced Henry Maxwell this morning as he preached against the liquor business and the damage it did to family life through the saloon. He had no new statements to make about the evil influence of the saloon in Raymond. What new facts were there? What could he say that had not been said by temperance orators a great many times? The effect of his message this morning owed its power to the unusual fact of his preaching about the saloon at all, together with the events that had stirred the people. He had never, in the course of his ten years' pastorate, mentioned the saloon as an enemy, not only to the poor and tempted, but to the business life of the community and the church itself. He spoke now with a freedom that seemed to measure his complete sense of conviction that Jesus would so speak.

At the close he pleaded with the people to remember the new life that had begun at the Rectangle. The regular election of city officers was near at hand. The question of license would be an issue in that election. What of the miserable individuals surrounded by the temptation of drink while just beginning to feel the joy of deliverance from sin? Was there one word to be said by the Christian disciple, businessman, citizen, in favor of continuing to license crime and shame-producing institutions? Was not the most Christian thing they could do as citizens to elect good men to city offices and clean up the municipality? What good were prayers to make Raymond better when votes and actions had really been on the side of the enemies of Jesus? What disciple would refuse to suffer or take up his cross in this matter?

His appeal was stronger at this last point than he knew. It is not too much to say that the spiritual tension of his people reached its highest point right there. The imitation of Jesus that had begun with a group of volunteers in the church was working like leaven through the whole church. Henry Maxwell would have been amazed if he could have measured the extent of desire on the part of his people to take up the cross.

While he was speaking this morning, before he closed with a loving appeal to the discipleship of two thousand years' knowledge of the Master, many a man and woman in the church was saying as Rachel had said so passionately to her mother, "I want to do something that will cost me in the way of sacrifice. I am hungry to suffer something for Jesus."

10

The service was over, the congregation had gone, and Maxwell again faced the company gathered in the lecture room as on the two previous Sundays. He had asked all to remain who had made the pledge of discipleship, and others who wished to be included. As he went in and faced the people there, his heart trembled. There were at least one hundred present. He missed Jasper Chase. But all the others were present. He asked Milton Wright to pray. The very air was charged with divine possibilities. Who could resist such a baptism of power? How had they lived all these years without it?

They counseled together, and there were many prayers. Henry Maxwell dated from that meeting some of the major events that afterward became a part of the history of the First Church and of Raymond. When finally they went home, all of them were filled with the Spirit's power.

Donald Marsh, president of Lincoln College, walked home with Mr. Maxwell.

"I have reached one conclusion, Maxwell," said Marsh, speaking slowly. "I have found my cross, and it is a heavy one; but I shall never be satisfied until I take it up and carry it."

Maxwell was silent, and the president went on. "Your sermon today made it clear to me what I ought to do. What would Jesus do in my place? I have asked the question repeatedly since I made my promise. I have tried to satisfy myself that He would simply go on as I have done, tending to the duties of my college, teaching the classes in ethics and philosophy. But I have not been able to avoid the feeling that He would do something more. That something is what I do not want to do. It will cause me genuine suffering to do it. I dread it with all my soul. You may be able to guess what it is?"

"Yes, I think I know. It is my cross, too. I would almost rather do anything else."

Donald Marsh looked surprised, then relieved. Then he spoke sadly, but with great conviction.

"Maxwell, you and I belong to a class of professional men who have always avoided the duties of citizenship. We have lived in a little world of literature and scholarly seclusion, doing work we have enjoyed and shrinking from the disagreeable duties that belong to the life of the average citizen. I confess with shame that I have purposely avoided the responsibility that I owe to this city personally. I understand that our city officials are a corrupt, unprincipled set of men, controlled in large part by the liquor element and thoroughly selfish so far as the affairs of city government are concerned. Yet all these years I, with nearly every teacher in the college, have been satisfied to let other men run the municipality and have lived in a little world of my own, out of touch and sympathy with the real world of people. 'What would Jesus do?' I have even tried to avoid an honest answer. I can no longer do so."

The tall, scholarly gentleman paused as they crossed a street. Then he continued: "My plain duty is to take a personal part in this coming election, go to the primaries, throw the weight of my influence, whatever it is, toward the nomination and election of good men, and plunge into the very depths of the entire horrible whirlpool of deceit, bribery, and political trickery as it exists in Raymond today. I would sooner walk up to the mouth of a cannon anytime than do this. I would give almost anything to be able to say, 'I do not believe Jesus would do anything of the sort.' But I am more and more persuaded that He would. I would so much prefer to remain quietly in my scholastic life with the classes in ethics and philosophy. But the call has come to me so plainly that I cannot escape: 'Donald Marsh, follow Me. Do your duty as a citizen of Raymond at the point where your citizenship will cost you something.' Maxwell, this is my cross. I must take it up or deny my Lord."

"You have spoken for me, also," replied Maxwell with a sad smile. "Why should I, simply because I am a minister, shelter myself behind my refined, sensitive feelings and, like a coward, refuse to touch the duty of citizenship except in a sermon? I am unused to the ways of the political life of the city. I have never taken an active part in any nomination of good men. There are hundreds of ministers like me. As a class we do not practice in the municipal life the duties and privileges we preach from the pulpit. What would Jesus do?

Like you, I am now at a point where I am driven to answer the question one way. My duty is plain. All my parish work, all my little trials or self-sacrifices as a pastor are as nothing compared with the breaking out of my scholarly, intellectual, self-contained habits into this open, coarse, public fight for a clean city life.

"I could go and live at the Rectangle for the rest of my life, and work in the slums for a bare living, and I could enjoy it more than the thought of plunging into a fight for the reform of this liquor-ridden city. It would cost me less. But like you, I have been unable to shake off my responsibility. We professional men—ministers, professors, artists, literary men, scholars—have almost invariably been political cowards. We have avoided the sacred duties of citizenship, either ignorantly or selfishly. Certainly Jesus in our age would not do that."

The two men walked on in silence for a while. Finally President Marsh said, "We do not need to act alone in this matter. With all the men who have made the promise, we certainly can have companionship and the strength of numbers. Let us organize the forces of good in Raymond for a battle against this corruption. We certainly ought to enter the primaries with a force that will be able to do more than voice a protest. Let us plan a campaign of organized righteousness. Jesus would use great wisdom in this matter. He would employ means. He would make large plans. Let us do likewise."

They continued talking a long time, and met again the next day in Maxwell's study to develop plans. The city primaries were set for that Friday. The primary called for a public meeting at the courthouse. Special officers to be nominated were mayor, city council, chief of police, city clerk, and city treasurer.

The Saturday edition of the *Evening News* gave a full account of the primaries, and in the editorial columns Edward Norman spoke with a directness and conviction that the many people in Raymond were learning to respect deeply, because it was so obviously sincere and unselfish. He said in part:

> It is safe to say that never before in the history of Raymond was there a primary like the one in the courthouse last night. It was, first of all, a complete surprise to the city politicians, who have been in the habit of carrying on the affairs of the city as if they owned it, with everyone else simply a tool or a cipher. To the amazement of the wire-pullers last night, a large number of the citizens of Raymond, who have heretofore taken no part in the city's affairs, entered the primary and controlled it, nominating men for all the offices to be filled at the coming election.
>
> It was a significant lesson in good citizenship. President Marsh of Lincoln College, who had never before entered a city primary and whose face was not even known to the ward politicians, made one of the best speeches ever heard in Raymond. When President Marsh rose to speak, many of these politicians asked, "Who is he?" Their consternation deepened as the primary proceeded, and it became evident that the old-time ring of city rulers was outnumbered.
>
> Rev. Henry Maxwell of the First Church, Milton Wright, Alexander Powers, Professors Brown, Willard, and Park of Lincoln College, Dr. West, Rev. George Maine of the Pilgrim Church, Dean Ward of the Holy Trinity, and scores

of well-known business and professional men were present. They had all come with the specific purpose of nominating the best men possible. Most of these men had never before participated in a primary. They were complete strangers to the politicians. But they had evidently profited by the politicians' methods and were able by organized and united effort to nominate their entire ticket.

As soon as it became plain that the primary was out of their control, the regular ring nominated another ticket. The *News* simply calls the attention of all decent citizens to the fact that this last ticket contains the names of men long controlled by the liquor interests of our town. The line is sharply and distinctly drawn between corrupt management, such as we have known for years, and the possibility of a clean, honest, capable, businesslike city administration, such as every good citizen ought to want.

It is not necessary to remind the people of Raymond that the question of local option comes up at the election. That will be the most important question on the ticket. The crisis of our city affairs has been reached. The issue is squarely before us. Shall we continue the rule of shameless incompetency, or shall we, as President Marsh said in his moving speech, rise as good citizens and begin a new order of things by the power of our ballot?

The *News* is positively and without reservation on the side of the new movement. We shall advocate the election of the men nominated by the majority of citizens who met in the first primary, and we call upon all lovers of decency, honesty, temperance, and the home to stand by President Marsh and the rest of the citizens who have thus begun a long-needed reform in our city.

President Marsh read this editorial and thanked God for Edward Norman. At the same time he understood well enough that every other paper in Raymond was on the other side. He did not underestimate the importance and seriousness of the fight that was only just begun. It was no secret that the *News* had lost enormously since it had been governed by the standard of "What would Jesus do?" The question now was, would the Christian people of Raymond stand by it? Would they make it possible for Norman to publish a daily Christian paper? Or would the desire for what is called "news" in the way of crime, scandal, political partisanship of the regular sort, and a dislike to champion so remarkable a reform in journalism influence them to drop the paper and refuse to give it their financial support?

That was, in fact, the question Edward Norman had asked when he wrote the Saturday editorial. He knew well enough that his action expressed in that editorial would cost him heavily from the hands of many businessmen of Raymond. And still as he drove his pen over the paper he asked another question: "What would Jesus do?" That question had become the force of his whole life now. It was greater than any other.

So for the first time in its history Raymond had seen its professional men, teachers, college professors, doctors, and ministers take political action and put themselves definitely and sharply in public antagonism to the forces that had long controlled the municipal government. This fact itself was astonishing. President Marsh acknowledged to himself with a feeling of humiliation that never before had he known what civic righteousness could accomplish. From that Friday night's work he dated for himself and his college a new definition of the worn phrase *the scholar of politics*. Education for him and those who were under his influence ever after meant the element of personal sacrifice.

At the Rectangle that week, the tide of spiritual life rose high, and as yet showed no signs of flowing back. Rachel and Virginia went every night. Virginia was rapidly reaching a conclusion with respect to a large part of her money. She had talked it over with Rachel, and they had been able to agree that if Jesus had a vast amount of money at his disposal, He might do with some of it as Virginia planned. They also agreed, however, that there could be no one fixed Christian way of using money. The rule that regulated its use was unselfishness.

But meanwhile the glory of the Spirit's power possessed all their best thought. Night after night that week they witnessed miracles as great as walking on the sea, or feeding the multitude with a few loaves and fishes. For what greater miracle is there than a regenerated human being? The transformation of these coarse, brutal lives into lovers of Jesus struck Rachel and Virginia with feelings no doubt similar to those who witnessed Lazarus walk out of the tomb.

Rollin Page came to all the meetings. There was no doubt of the change that had come over him. He was unusually quiet. He talked more with Mr. Gray than with anyone else. He did not avoid Rachel, but he seemed reluctant to renew his relationship with her. Rachel found it even difficult to express to him her pleasure at the new life he had commenced. Rollin seemed to have withdrawn until he could adjust to his new life.

The end of the week found the Rectangle struggling hard between two mighty opposing forces. The Holy Spirit was battling against the raw evil that so long had held a jealous grasp on its slaves. If the Christian people of Raymond could have realized what the contest meant to the souls newly awakened to a purer life, it would not seem possible that the election could result in the old system of license. But the issue was in doubt. Meanwhile, the horror of the daily surroundings of many of the converts was slowly burning its way into the knowledge of Virginia and Rachel, and every night as they went uptown to their fine homes, they carried heavy hearts.

"A good many of those poor creatures will slip back again," the evangelist would say with a sadness too deep for tears. "The environment is too great an obstacle. O Lord! How long shall Christian people continue to support by their silence and their ballots the greatest form of slavery now known in America?"

11

Saturday afternoon Virginia was just stepping out of her house to go and see Rachel and talk over her new plans, when a carriage drove up containing three of her friends. Virginia went out to the driveway and stood talking with them. They had come only to make a casual call and ask her to go with them up on the boulevard. There was to be a band concert in the park and it was a beautiful day.

"Where have you been all this time, Virginia?" asked one of the young women curiously. "We hear that you have gone into show business. Tell us about it."

Virginia was irritated but after a moment's hesitation she frankly told something of her experience at the Rectangle. Her friends in the carriage became really interested.

"I tell you, girls, let's go slumming with Virginia this afternoon instead of going to the band concert I've never been down to the Rectangle. I've heard it's a really wicked place with lots to see. Virginia will act as a guide, and it will be real"—fun, she was going to say, but Virginia's look made her substitute the word *interesting*.

Virginia was angry. At first she said to herself that she would not go under such circumstances. But when all the women showed such earnestness, she hesitated.

Suddenly she saw in the idle curiosity an opportunity. They had never seen the sin and misery of Raymond. Why should they not see it, even if their motive in going there was simply to pass away an afternoon?

"Very well, I'll go with you. But when we get to the Rectangle, you must do exactly what I tell you." And Virginia entered the carriage with her friends.

"Shouldn't we take a policeman along?" asked one of the women with a nervous laugh. "It really isn't safe down there, you know."

"There's no danger," said Virginia briefly.

"Is it true that your brother Rollin has been converted?" asked one of her friends, looking at Virginia curiously. It impressed her during the drive to the Rectangle that all three of them were regarding her with close attention, as if she were peculiar.

"Yes, he certainly is."

"I understand he is going around to the clubs talking with his old friends there, preaching to them. Doesn't that seem funny?" asked another.

Virginia did not answer. The three young women were beginning to feel sober as the carriage turned into the street leading to the Rectangle. As they neared the district they grew more and more nervous. The sights and smells and sounds that had become familiar to Virginia struck the senses of these refined, delicate society women as something horrible. As they entered into the district, the Rectangle seemed to stare with a bleary, beer-soaked countenance at this fine carriage with its load of fashionably dressed young ladies. "Slumming" has never been a fad with Raymond society, and this was perhaps the first time that the two had come together in this way. Virginia's friends felt that instead of seeing the Rectangle they were being made the objects of curiosity. They were frightened and disgusted.

"Let's go back. I've seen enough," said the one who was sitting with Virginia.

They were at that moment just opposite a notorious saloon and gambling house. The street was narrow and the sidewalk crowded. Suddenly, out of the door of the saloon a young woman reeled. She was singing, in a broken, drunken sob, "Just as I am, without one plea," and as the carriage rolled past she raised her face so that Virginia saw it clearly. It was the face of the woman who had knelt sobbing that night with Virginia kneeling beside her and praying for her.

"Stop!" cried Virginia, motioning to the driver. The carriage stopped, and in a moment she was out and had gone up to the girl and taken her by the arm.

"Loreen," she began and that was all. The girl looked into Virginia's face, and her expression changed into a look of utter horror. The ladies in the carriage stared with astonishment. The saloon-keeper had come to the door and was standing there looking on, with his hands on his hips. Residents of the Rectangle—from its windows, its saloons, its filthy sidewalks—paused, and with undisguised wonder stared at the two women. Over the scene the warm sun of spring poured its mellow warmth. A faint breath of music from the bandstand in the central park of Raymond floated into the Rectangle. The concert had begun. Listeners would include the fashion and wealth of Raymond.

When Virginia left the carriage and went up to Loreen, she had no definite idea as to what she would do or what the result of her action would be. She simply saw a soul that had tasted the joy of a better life slipping back again into its old hell of shame and filth. And before she had touched the drunken girl's arm, she had asked herself only one question, "What would Jesus do?"

Then she turned to her friends, "Drive on. Don't wait for me! I am going to see my friend home."

The other women were speechless.

"Go on! I cannot go back with you," said Virginia.

The driver started the horses slowly. One of the ladies leaned a little out of the carriage.

"Can't we—that is—do you want our help? Couldn't you—"

"No, no!" exclaimed Virginia. "You cannot be of any help to me."

The carriage moved on and Virginia was alone with her charge.

She looked up and around. Many faces in the crowd were sympathetic. They were not all cruel or brutal. The Holy Spirit had softened a good deal of the Rectangle.

"Where does she live?" asked Virginia.

No one answered. It occurred to Virginia afterward, when she had time to think it over, that the Rectangle showed a

118

delicacy in its sad silence that would have done credit to the boulevard.

The girl suddenly wrenched her arm from Virginia's grasp. In doing so she nearly threw Virginia down.

"You shall not touch me," she exclaimed hoarsely. "Leave me. Let me go to hell. That's where I belong. The devil is waiting for me. See him!" She turned and pointed with a shaking finger at the saloon-keeper. The crowd laughed.

Virginia stepped up to her and put her arm about her. "Loreen," she said firmly, "come with me. You do not belong to hell. You belong to Jesus, and He will save you. Come."

The girl suddenly burst into tears. She was only partly sobered by the shock of meeting Virginia.

Virginia looked around again. "Where does Mr. Gray live?" she asked. She knew that the evangelist boarded somewhere near that tent.

A number of voices gave the direction.

"Come, Loreen, I want you to go with me to Mr. Gray's," she said, still keeping her hold of the swaying, trembling creature who moaned and sobbed and now clung to Virginia.

So the two moved on through the Rectangle toward the evangelist's lodging place. The sight seemed to impress the Rectangle. It never took itself seriously when it was drunk; but this was different. Seeing Loreen stumbling through the gutter dead drunk would make the Rectangle laugh and jest. But Loreen staggering along with a young, well-dressed woman supporting her, was something else. The Rectangle viewed this with soberness and more or less wondering admiration.

When they finally reached Mr. Gray's lodging place, the woman who answered Virginia's knock said that both Mr. and Mrs. Gray were out somewhere and would not be back until six o'clock.

Virginia had not planned anything farther than a possible appeal to the Grays either to take charge of Loreen for a while, or find some safe place for her until she was sober. She stood now at the door somewhat at a loss to know what to do. Loreen sank down stupidly on the steps and buried her face in her arms. Virginia eyed the miserable figure of the girl with sensations she was afraid would grow into disgust.

Finally a thought possessed her that she could not escape. What was to hinder her taking Loreen home with her? Why should not this homeless, wretched creature be cared for in Virginia's own home, instead of being consigned to strangers in some hospital or house of charity? Virginia really knew very little about such places of refuge. As a matter of fact, there were two or three such institutions in Raymond; but it is doubtful if any of them would have taken a person like Loreen in her present condition. But that was not the question with Virginia just now. "What would Jesus do with Loreen?" was what Virginia faced, and she finally answered it by touching the girl again.

"Loreen, come. You are going home with me."

Loreen staggered to her feet, and to Virginia's surprise, made no trouble. She had expected resistance or a stubborn refusal to move. When they reached the corner and took the streetcar, it was nearly full of people going uptown. Virginia was painfully conscious of the stares that greeted her and her companion as they entered. But her thoughts were directed more and more to the approaching scene with her grandmother. What would Madame Page say?

Loreen was nearly sober now. But she was lapsing into a state of stupor. Virginia was obliged to hold fast to her arm. Several times the girl lurched heavily against her, and as the two went up the avenue people turned and gazed at them. When she mounted the steps of her handsome house, Virginia breathed a sigh of relief, even in the face of the interview with her grandmother. And when the door shut and she was in the wide hall with her homeless outcast, she felt equal to anything that might now come.

Madame Page was in the library. Hearing Virginia come in, she strode into the hall. Virginia stood there supporting Loreen, who stared at the richness and magnificence of the furnishings around her.

"Grandmother"—Virginia spoke without hesitation and very clearly—"this is Loreen. She is one of my friends from the Rectangle. She is in trouble and has no home. I am going to take care of her here for the time being."

Madame Page glanced from her granddaughter to Loreen in astonishment.

"Did you say she is one of your friends?" she asked in a cold, sarcastic voice that hurt Virginia more than anything she had yet felt.

"Yes, I said so." Virginia's face flushed, but she recalled the phrase that Mr. Gray had used for one of his recent sermons. *A friend of publicans and sinners.* Surely Jesus would do as she was doing.

"Do you know what this girl is?" asked Madame Page in an angry whisper, stepping near Virginia.

"I know very well. She is an outcast. You need not tell me, Grandmother. She is drunk at this minute. But she is also a child of God. I have seen her on her knees in repentance. And I have seen hell reach out its fingers after her again. By the grace of Christ, I feel that the least I can do is to rescue her from this. Grandmother, we call ourselves Christians. Here is a poor, lost creature without a home, slipping back into a life of misery, and we have more than enough. I have brought her here and I shall keep her."

Madame Page glared at Virginia and clenched her hands. All this was contrary to her social code of conduct. What would Virginia's action cost the family in the way of criticism and the loss of standing, and all that long list of necessary relationships which people of wealth and position must sustain to be the leaders of society? To Madame Page, society was a power to be feared and obeyed. The loss of its good will was a loss more to be dreaded than anything, except the loss of wealth itself.

Fully aroused and determined, Madame Page stood erect and sternly confronted Virginia. Meanwhile, Virginia had placed her arm about Loreen and calmly looked her grandmother in the face.

"You shall not do this, Virginia. You can send her to the asylum for helpless women. We can pay all the expenses. But we cannot afford, for the sake of our reputations, to shelter such a person here in our home."

"Grandmother, I do not wish to do anything that is

displeasing to you, but I must keep Loreen here tonight and longer, if it seems best."

"Then you can answer for the consequences! I will not stay in the same house with a miserable—" Virginia stopped her before she could speak the next word.

"Grandmother, this house belongs to me. It is your home, too, as long as you choose to remain. But in this matter I must act as I fully believe Jesus would. I am willing to bear all that society may say or do. Society is not my God. By the side of this woman in need, I do not consider the verdict of society as of any value."

"I shall not remain here, then," said Madame Page. She turned suddenly and walked to the end of the hall, then stopped, turned, and glared at Virginia.

"You can always remember that you have driven your grandmother out of your house in favor of a drunken woman." Then, without waiting for Virginia to reply, she turned again and went upstairs.

Virginia found Loreen a room and helped her into bed. She was fast lapsing into unconsciousness. During the brief scene in the hall, she had clung to Virginia so hard that her arm was sore from the clutch of the girl's fingers.

Virginia did not know whether her grandmother would leave the house or not. The elderly woman had abundant means of her own, was perfectly well and vigorous and capable of caring for herself. She had sisters and brothers living in the South, and was in the habit of spending several weeks each year with them. Virginia was not anxious about her welfare, as far as that went; but the interview had been a painful one. Going over it, however, she found little cause for regret. There was no question in her mind that she had done the right thing.

Retiring to her room, Virginia spent the rest of the afternoon in thought and meditation. A little before the dinner hour she went downstairs. Madame Page was not there. A few minutes later Rollin came in bringing word that his grandmother had taken the evening train for the South. She had told him her reason for going.

"Rollin," said Virginia, realizing for the first time how much her brother's changed life meant to her, "am I wrong?"

"No, I cannot believe you are. It's an awkward situation, of course, but if you think this poor creature owes her safety and salvation to your personal care, it is the only thing for you to do."

And so Rollin comforted Virginia and counseled with her that evening. And in watching her brother's changed demeanor, Virginia rejoiced. Old things had passed away. Truly all things had become new through Jesus Christ.

Dr. West came that evening at Virginia's request and examined Loreen. The best that could be given her, he reported, was quiet nursing and careful watching and personal love. So in a beautiful room, where hanging on the wall was a picture of Christ walking by the sea, the bewildered outcast began her recuperation.

In another bedroom, Virginia wondered a bit apprehensively what Jesus would have her do next.

12

Meanwhile, the Rectangle awaited the issue of the election with more interest than usual. And Mr. Gray and his wife wept over the pitiful individuals who, after a struggle with surroundings that daily tempted them, too often wearied of the battle and went whirling over the cataract into the boiling abyss of their previous condition.

The Sunday after-meeting at the First Church was now well established and eagerly attended. Henry Maxwell went into the lecture room on the Sunday following the week of the primary, and was greeted with an enthusiasm that made him tremble. He noted again the absence of Jasper Chase, plus two others, but all the rest were present and they seemed drawn close together by a bond of common fellowship. Out of this was coming the realization that the spirit of Jesus was a Spirit of very open, frank confession of experience.

It seemed the most natural thing in the world, therefore, for Edward Norman to be telling all the rest of the group about the details of his newspaper.

"The fact is, I have lost a good deal of money during the last three weeks. I cannot tell just how much. I am losing many subscribers every day."

"What do the subscribers give as their reason for dropping the paper?" asked Mr. Maxwell.

"There are a good many different reasons. Some say they want a paper that prints all the news; meaning by that, the crime details, sensations like prizefights, scandals and horrors of various kinds. Others object to the discontinuance of the Sunday edition. I have lost hundreds of subscribers by that action, although I have made satisfactory arrangements with many of the old subscribers by giving them even more in the extra Saturday edition than they formerly had in the Sunday issue. The loss of advertising revenue has hurt a lot.

"But taking a stand on political questions has probably cost me more than any other. The bulk of my subscribers are intensely partisan. I may as well tell you all frankly that if I continue to follow the plan that I honestly believe Jesus would pursue in the matter of political issues and their treatment from a nonpartisan and moral standpoint, the *News* will soon not be able to pay its operating expenses. There is only one hope for the paper, as I see it."

He paused a moment, and the room was very quiet. Then he continued, "That one hope is the Christian people in Raymond. Assuming that the *News* has lost heavily from cancellations by people who do not care for a Christian daily, and from others who simply look upon a newspaper as a purveyor of all sorts of material to amuse and interest them—are there enough Christian people in Raymond who will rally to the support of a paper such as Jesus could presumably edit? Or are the habits of the church people so firmly established in their demands for standard journalism that they will not subscribe to a paper that attempts to deal with issues from both a Christian and moral viewpoint?

"As I understand the promise we made, we were not to ask any questions about, 'Will it pay?' but all our action was to be based on the one question 'What would Jesus do?' After my three weeks' experience, I'm convinced that most businessmen would lose vast sums of money if this rule of Jesus were honestly applied. And unless the Christian people of Raymond, the church members and professing disciples, will support the paper with subscriptions and advertisements, I cannot continue its publication on the present basis."

"Do you mean that a Christian daily ought to be endowed with a large sum, like a Christian college, in order to make it pay?" Virginia asked with intense interest.

"That is exactly what I mean. I have laid out plans for putting into the *News* such a variety of material, in such a strong and truly interesting way, that it would more than make up for whatever was absent from its columns in the way of non-Christian matter. But my plans call for a large outlay of money. I am confident that a Christian daily, such as Jesus would approve and containing only what He would print, can be made to succeed financially if it is planned on the right lines. But it will take a large sum of money to work out the plans."

"How much do you think?" asked Virginia quietly.

Edward Norman looked at her keenly, and his face flushed a moment, as an idea of her purpose crossed his mind. He had known her when she was a little girl in the Sunday school, and he had been in intimate business relations with her father.

"I should say a half-million dollars in a town like Raymond would be needed in the establishment of a paper such as we have in mind," he answered.

"Then," said Virginia, speaking as if the thought were fully considered, "I am ready to put that amount of money into the paper—on the one condition, of course, that it be carried on as it has been begun."

Startled by Virginia's offer, the editor was speechless for a moment. But Virginia had more to say.

"Dear friends," she went on, with sadness in her voice, "I do not want any of you to credit me with an act of great generosity. I have come to know lately that the money I have called my own is not my own, but God's. If I, as a steward of His, see some wise way to invest His money, it is not an occasion for praise or thanks from anyone simply because I have proved honest in my administration of the funds He had asked me to use for His glory. I have been thinking of doing something like this for some time. The fact is that in our coming political fight against corruption in Raymond—and it has only just begun—we shall need the *News* to champion the Christian side.

"You all know that all the other papers are for the entrenched interests. As long as the liquor problems exists, the work of the mission at the Rectangle is carried on at a terrible disadvantage. What can Mr. Gray do with his Gospel meetings when half his converts are drinking people, daily tempted and enticed by a saloon on every corner? It would be giving up to the enemy to allow the *News* to fail. I have great confidence in Mr. Norman's ability. I have not seen his plans; but I have the same confidence that he has in making the paper succeed, if it is carried forward on a large enough scale. I believe what I am doing is what Jesus would do."

No one spoke for a while. Mr. Maxwell standing there, where the faces lifted their intense gaze into his, felt what he had often felt before—a strange but vivid change of setting, back to the first century, when the disciples had all things in common and a powerful spirit of fellowship flowed freely between them. How little his church membership had known of this fellowship until this small group had begun to do as they believed Jesus would do!

He felt the development of unspoken comradeship such as they had never known before. It was present with them while Virginia was speaking and during the silence that followed. If he had to define the common feeling it would go like this: "In the course of my obedience to my promise, if I should meet with loss or trouble in the world, I can depend upon the genuine, practical sympathy and fellowship of any other Christian in this room who has with me made the pledge to do all things by the rule 'What would Jesus do?'"

An overwhelming love for his people swept over Henry Maxwell. They were developing the kind of trust in their Lord that the early disciples had as they faced loss and death with courage and even joy.

Before the group broke up, there were several confidences like those of Edward Norman. Two young men told the loss of jobs owing to their honest obedience to their promise.

Alexander Powers reported that the Commission had promised to take action on his evidence at the earliest possible date. He was engaged at his old work of telegraphy. It was significant that since resigning his position, neither his wife nor daughter had appeared in public. No one but himself knew the depth of that family estrangement and misunderstanding of his higher motive. Yet many of the disciples present in the meeting carried similar burdens. These were things they could not talk about.

Henry Maxwell, from his knowledge of his people, concluded that obedience to their pledge had resulted in emotional upsets and even strife in many a home. Truly "a man's foes are they of his own household," when the rule of Jesus is obeyed by some and disobeyed by others. Jesus is a great divider of life. It seemed that one must walk parallel with Him or directly across His way.

Compensating for these problems, however, was the tide of fellowship which arose for one another. Maxwell watched it, trembling for its climax, which he knew was not yet reached. When it was, where would it lead them? He did not know, but he was not unduly alarmed about it. He only watched with growing wonder the results of that simple promise as it was being obeyed in these various lives. The results were already being felt all over the city. Who could measure their influence at the end of a year?

One practical form of this fellowship showed itself in the assurances that Edward Norman received of support for his paper. There was a general flocking toward him when the meeting closed, and the response to his appeal for help from the Christian disciples in Raymond was fully understood by this little company.

The value of such a paper in the homes and in behalf of good citizenship, especially in the present crisis in the city, could not be measured. It remained to be seen what could be done now that the paper was endowed so liberally. But it still was true, as Edward Norman insisted, that money alone could not make the paper a power. It must receive the support and sympathy of the Christians in Raymond before it could be counted as one of the great forces of the city.

The week that followed this Sunday meeting was one of great excitement in Raymond. It was the week of the election. President Marsh, true to his promise, tore himself out of the scholarly seclusion of years. The pain and anguish he experienced cost him more than anything he had ever before done as a follower of Christ. With him were a few of the college professors who had made the pledge in the First Church. Their experience and suffering were the same as his; for their isolation from all duties of citizenship had been the same.

The same was also true of Henry Maxwell, who plunged into the horror of this fight against the liquor forces with a sickening dread of each day's new encounter. For never before had he borne such a cross. He staggered under it, and in the brief intervals when he came in from the work and sought the quiet of his study for rest, sweat broke out on his forehead and he felt the actual terror of one who marches into unseen, unknown horrors. He was not a coward; but he felt a dread that any man of his habits feels when confronted suddenly with a duty which carries with it the doing of certain things so unfamiliar that the actual details connected with it betray his ignorance and fill him with the shame of humiliation.

Saturday, election day, arrived, and the excitement rose to its height. An attempt was made to close all the saloons. It was only partly successful. There was a great deal of drinking going on all day. The Rectangle boiled and heaved and cursed and turned its worst side out to the gaze of the city. Mr. Gray had continued his meetings during the week, and the results had been even greater than he had dared to hope. When Saturday came, it seemed to him that the crisis in his work had been reached. The forces of good and evil were in desperate conflict.

The more interest in the meetings, the more ferocity and vileness outside. The saloon men no longer concealed their feelings. Open threats of violence were made. Once during the week Gray and his little company of helpers were assailed with dirt, rocks, and garbage as they left the tent late at night. The police sent down a special force, and Virginia and Rachel were always under the protection of either Rollin or Dr. West. Rachel's power in song had not diminished. Rather, with each night it seemed to add to the intensity and reality of the Spirit's presence.

At first the evangelist hesitated to have a meeting on election night. But he had a simple rule of action and was always guided by it. In this situation the Spirit seemed to lead him to continue the meeting, and so Saturday the tent meeting went on as usual.

The excitement all over the city had reached its climax when the polls closed at six o'clock. Never before had there been such a contest in Raymond. The issue of license or no license had never been up for vote under such circumstances. Never before had such contrasting elements in the city been arrayed against each other. It was an unheard-of thing for the president of Lincoln College, the pastor of the First Church, the dean of the cathedral, the professional men living in the fine houses on the boulevard, to come personally into the wards and, by their presence and their example, represent the Christian conscience of the community. The ward politicians were astonished at the sight.

However, their astonishment did not prevent their activity. The fight grew hotter every hour; and when six o'clock came neither side could have guessed at the result with any certainty.

It was after ten when the meeting at the tent was closed. It had been a strange, and in some respects a remarkable, meeting. Maxwell had come down again, at Gray's request. He was completely worn out by the day's work, but the appeal from Gray came to him in such a form that he did not feel able to resist it. President Marsh was also present. He had never been to the Rectangle, and his curiosity was aroused over the growing influence of the evangelist's work in the worst part of the city.

Dr. West and Rollin arrived with Rachel, Virginia, and Loreen, who now lived with Virginia. The latter stayed near the organ. She was sober, but possessed a humility and dread of herself that kept her as close to Virginia as a faithful dog.

All through the service Loreen sat with bowed heard, quietly weeping most of the time; actually sobbing when Rachel sang the song "I Was a Wandering Sheep." She listened to prayer, appeal, and confession all about her like one who was a part of a new creation, yet fearful of her right to share in it fully.

The tent had been crowded. The noise outside had increased as the night advanced, and Gray thought it wise not to prolong the service. Once in a while a loud cry swept into the tent. The returns from the election were beginning to come in, and the Rectangle had emptied every lodging-house, den, and hovel into the streets.

In spite of these distractions, Rachel's singing kept the crowd in the tent from dissolving. There were a dozen or more conversions. Finally the people became restless and Gray closed the service, remaining a while with the converts.

Rachel, Virginia, Loreen, Rollin, President Marsh, Mr. Maxwell, and Dr. West went out together, intending to walk to the usual waiting place for their streetcar. As they came out of the tent, they were at once aware that the Rectangle was trembling on the verge of a drunken riot, and as they pushed through the gathering mobs in the narrow streets they began to realize that they themselves were objects of special attention.

"There he is, the bloke in the tall hat. He's the leader!" shouted a rough voice. President Marsh with his erect, commanding figure, was conspicuous in the little company.

"How has the election gone? It is too early to know the result yet, isn't it?" He asked the question aloud, and a man answered, "They say second and third wards have gone almost solid for no license. If that is so, the whisky interests have been beaten."

"I hope it is true," exclaimed Maxwell. "Marsh, we are in danger here. We ought to get the ladies to a place of safety."

"That is true," said Marsh gravely. At that moment a shower of garbage pelted them. The narrow street and sidewalk in front of them was completely choked with the worst elements of the Rectangle.

"This looks serious," said Maxwell. With Marsh, Rollin, and Dr. West he started to go forward through the small opening. Virginia, Rachel, and Loreen followed close, sheltered by the men, who now realized something of their danger. The Rectangle was drunk and enraged. It saw in Marsh and Maxwell two of the leaders in the election contest who had perhaps robbed them of their saloon.

"Down with the aristocrats!" shouted a shrill voice more like a woman's than a man's.

A shower of mud and stones followed. Rachel remembered afterward that Rollin jumped directly in front of her and received on his head and chest a number of missiles that would probably have struck her if he had not shielded her from them.

Just then, before the police reached them, Loreen darted forward in front of Virginia and pushed her aside with a scream. Out of the upper window of a room over the very saloon where Loreen had been the week before, someone had thrown a heavy bottle. It struck Loreen on the head and she fell to the ground. Virginia turned and instantly knelt down by her. Police officers by this time had reached the little company.

President Marsh raised his arm and shouted over the howl that was beginning to rise from the mob: "Stop! You've killed a woman!"

The announcement partly sobered the crowd.

"Is it true?" Henry Maxwell asked, as Dr. West knelt on the other side of Loreen, supporting her.

"She's dying!" said Dr. West briefly.

Loreen opened her eyes and smiled at Virginia, who wiped the blood from her face, then bent over and kissed her. Loreen smiled again, and the next moment she was gone.

13

The body of Loreen lay in state in the Page mansion. It was Sunday morning, and the clear, sweet air of late spring was just beginning to breathe over the city. The perfume of early blossoms in the woods and fields swept over the casket from one of the open windows at the end of the grand hall. The church bells were ringing and the people on the avenue going by to Sunday church services directed curious, inquiring looks up at the great house and then went on, talking of the recent events that had made history in the city.

At First Church, Mr. Maxwell, bearing on his face marks of the scene he had been through the night before, confronted an immense congregation. He spoke to it with a passion and a power that came naturally out of the profound experiences of the day before. Yet through his impassioned words this morning there was a note of sadness and rebuke that turned many of the members pale with self-accusation or inward anger.

For Raymond had awakened that morning to the fact that the city had gone for the licensing of liquor after all. The rumor at the Rectangle that the second and third wards had voted for no license proved to be false. It was true that the victory was won by a meager majority, but the result was the same as if it had been overwhelming. Raymond had voted to continue the saloon another year. The Christians of Raymond stood condemned by the result. Hundreds of Christians had failed to go to the polls, and many more than that number had voted with the whisky interests. If all the church members of Raymond had voted against the saloon, it would have been outlawed instead of crowned king of the municipality. That had been the fact in Raymond for years. The saloon ruled.

Then the pastor told the story of Loreen, brutally struck down by the very hand that had led her toward an alcoholic existence. Meanwhile the saloon, which so many Christian people of Raymond voted to support, would open its doors tomorrow and damn with earthly and eternal destruction a hundred Loreens before the year had drawn to its close.

All this, with a voice that rang and trembled, did Henry Maxwell pour out upon his people that Sunday morning. And men and women wept as he spoke. President Marsh sat there, his usual erect, handsome, firm, self-confident bearing all gone; his head bowed upon his breast; great tears rolling down his cheek, unmindful of the fact that never before had he shown outward emotion in a public service.

Nearby Edward Norman sat erect, his clear-cut, keen face looking straight ahead. But his lips trembled and he clutched the end of the pew with deep emotion. No man had given or suffered more to influence public opinion that last week than Norman. The thought that the Christian conscience had been aroused too late or too feebly lay with a weight of accusation upon the heart of the editor. What if long ago he had begun to do as Jesus would have done? Who could tell what might have been accomplished by this time?

And up in the choir, Rachel Winslow gave way to feelings that had never before mastered her. When Mr. Maxwell finished and she tried to sing the closing solo after the prayer, her voice broke, and for the first time in her life she was obliged to sit down, unable emotionally to go on.

Over the church, in the silence that followed this unusual scene, the sounds of weeping arose. When had the First Church yielded to such a baptism of tears? What had become of its regular, precise, conventional order of service, undisturbed by any unseemly emotion and unmoved by any foolish excitement? But the people had lately had their deepest convictions touched. They had been living so long on their surface feelings that they had almost forgotten the deeper springs of life. Now that these had broken to the surface, the people were convicted of the meaning of their discipleship.

Mr. Maxwell did not ask this morning for volunteers to join those who had already pledged to do as Jesus would. But when the congregation had finally gone and he had entered the lecture room, it took but a glance to show him that the original company of followers had been largely increased. The meeting was tender; it glowed with the Spirit's presence. It was alive with strong and lasting revolve to begin a new war on the entrenched political power of Raymond that would break its reign.

Since that first Sunday when the first company of volunteers had pledged themselves to do as Jesus would do, the meetings had been characterized by different impulses or impressions. Today the entire force of the gathering seemed to be directed to this one large purpose. It was a meeting full of broken prayers, of contrition, of confession, of strong yearning for a new and better civic life. And all through it ran the one general cry for deliverance from the awful curse of the saloon.

But if the First Church was deeply stirred by the events of the last week, the Rectangle also felt moved strongly in its own way. The death of Loreen was not in itself so remarkable a fact. It was her recent acquaintance with the people from the city that lifted her into special prominence and surrounded her death with more than ordinary importance. Everyone in the Rectangle knew that Loreen was at this moment lying in the Page mansion up on the avenue. Exaggerated reports of the magnificence of the casket had already furnished material for eager gossip. The Rectangle was excited to know the details of the funeral. Would it be public? Whom did Miss Page intend to invite? The Rectangle had never before mingled even in this distant personal manner with the aristocracy on the boulevard. The opportunities for doing so were not frequent. Mr. Gray and his wife were besieged by inquiries wanting to know what Loreen's friends and acquaintances were expected to do in paying their last respects to her. For her acquaintance was large and many of the recent converts were among her friends.

To make a decision about the funeral, Mr. and Mrs. Gray and Henry Maxwell met with Virginia Page at her home.

"I am and always have been opposed to large public funerals," said Mr. Gray, whose simplicity of character was one of his great sources of strength. "But the plea of those people who knew Loreen is so earnest that I cannot refuse their desire to see her and pay this last little honor to her poor body. What do you think, Mr. Maxwell? I will be guided by your judgment in the matter. I am sure that whatever you and Miss Page decide will be right."

"I feel as you do," replied Mr. Maxwell. "Under most circumstances I have a great distaste for what seems like public display at such times. But this seems different. The people at the Rectangle will not come to a service in my church. I think the most Christian thing will be to let them have the service at the tent. How do you feel about it, Virginia?"

"I agree," said Virginia sadly. "Dear Loreen, I am overwhelmed when I think of how she gave her life for mine. Let her friends be allowed the gratification of their wishes."

So with some difficulty arrangements were made to hold the service at the tent. Virginia, with her uncle and Rollin, accompanied by Maxwell, Rachel and President Marsh, plus the quartet from the First Church, went down and witnessed one of the strangest events of their lives.

It happened that a noted newspaper correspondent was passing through Raymond that afternoon on his way to an editorial convention in a neighboring city. He had heard of the unusual goings-on in Raymond, the death of Loreen, and that the service would be held in the tent, and he decided to attend. His description of it caught the attention of many readers throughout the country:

There was a unique funeral service held in Raymond this afternoon in the tent of an evangelist, Rev. John Gray, down in a slum district known as the Rectangle. It was for a woman, Loreen Carson, killed during an election riot last Saturday night. Miss Carson had been recently converted during the evangelist's meetings and was struck and killed by a bottle thrown from a window while returning from one of the meetings in company with other converts and some of her friends. Though a drunkard and for years known as a woman of the street, the services for Miss Carson were as impressive as any I ever witnessed in a metropolitan church for a distinguished citizen.

First, a most exquisite anthem was sung by a trained choir. I was astonished to hear voices like those one expects to hear only in great churches or at important concerts. But the most remarkable part of the music was a solo sung by a strikingly beautiful young woman, Rachel Winslow, who I understand has been sought by the National Opera, and who for some reason refused to accept an offer to go on the stage. Everybody was weeping before she had sung two dozen words. Miss Winslow sings in the First Church of Raymond, and could probably command a huge salary as a concert artist. She will probably be heard from soon. Such a voice could win its way anywhere.

The funeral service, too, was remarkable. Evangelist John Gray, a man of unassuming style, said a few words and he was followed by the Rev. Henry Maxwell, pastor of the First Church of Raymond. Mr. Maxwell spoke of the dead woman and her decision for Christ. Then he related in an eloquent manner how the liquor business destroyed the lives of men and women. Raymond, being a railroad town and the center of the packing interests for this region, is full of saloons. I caught from the minister's remarks that he had only recently changed his views in regard to license.

Then followed what was perhaps the most unusual part of this strange service. The women in the tent, at least a large part of them up near the coffin, began to sing in a soft, tearful way "I Was a Wandering Sheep."

While the singing was going on, the row of women stood up and walked slowly past the casket, and as they went by, each one placed a flower of some kind on it. Then they sat down and another row filed past, leaving their flowers. All the time the singing continued softly, like rain on a tent cover when the wind is gentle. It was at once one of the simplest and one of the most impressive sights I have ever witnessed.

The sides of the tent were up, and hundreds of people who could not get in stood outside, all as still as death itself, with wonderful sadness and solemnity for such a rough-looking people. There must have been a hundred of these women, and I was told that many of them had been converted at recent meetings. I cannot describe the effect of that singing. Not a man sang a note. All you heard were women's voices, so soft and yet so distinct that the effect was startling.

The service closed with another solo by Miss Winslow, who sang "There Were Ninety and Nine." And then the evangelist asked them all to bow their heads while he prayed. In order to catch my train, I had to leave during the prayer, but the last view I caught of the scene as the train moved out of the station was of the great crowd pouring from the tent and forming in open ranks while the coffin was borne out by six of the women. It is a long time since I have seen such a moving picture in this unpoetical republic.

If Loreen's funeral impressed a passing stranger like this, it is not difficult to imagine the profound feelings of those who had been intimately connected with her life and death. Nothing had ever entered the Rectangle that had moved it so deeply as Loreen's body in that coffin. And the Holy Spirit seemed to bless with special power the use of this lifeless form; for that night He swept more than a score of lost souls, mostly women, into God's Kingdom.

The saloon, from whose window Loreen had been killed, was formally closed Monday and Tuesday, while the authorities arrested the proprietor who was charged with the murder. But nothing could be proved against anyone, so before Saturday the saloon was running as regularly as ever. And the forces of law were never able to bring anyone to conviction for the murder of Loreen.

No one in all Raymond, including the Rectangle, felt Loreen's death more keenly than Virginia. It came as a distinct personal loss to her. That short week while Loreen had been in her home had opened Virginia's heart to a new life. She was talking it over with Rachel the day after the funeral. They were sitting in the hall of the Page mansion.

"I am going to do something with my money to help these women to a better life," said Virginia, looking over to the end of the hall where, the day before, Loreen's body had lain. "I have decided on a good plan, as it seems to me. I have talked it over with Rollin. He will devote a large part of his money also to the same plan."

"How much money have you, Virginia, to give in this way?" asked Rachel. Once she would never have asked such a personal question. Now it seemed as natural to talk frankly about money as about anything else that belonged to God.

"I have available for use at least 450 thousand dollars. Rollin has as much more. It is one of his bitter regrets now that his extravagant habits of life before his conversion dissipated nearly half of what Father left him. We are both eager to make all the reparation in our power. What would Jesus do with this money? We want to answer that question honestly and wisely. The money I shall put into the *News* is, I am confident, in line with His probable action. It is as necessary that we have a daily Christian paper in Raymond as it is to have a church or a college. I am satisfied that the half-million dollars going to Mr. Norman will be a powerful factor in Raymond to serve Christ.

"About my other plan, Rachel, I want you to work with me. Rollin and I are going to buy up a large part of the property in the Rectangle. The field where the tent now is located has been in litigation for years. We mean to secure the entire tract as soon as the courts have settled the title. For some time I have been making a special study of the various methods of Christian church work in the heart of great city slums. I do not know that I have yet been able to tell just what is the wisest and most effective kind of work that can be done in Raymond.

"But I do know this much. My money—I mean God's, which He wants me to use—can build wholesome lodging-houses, refuges for poor women, asylums for shop girls, safety for many a lost girl like Loreen. And I do not want to be simply a dispenser of this money. God help me! I want to put myself into the project.

"And now, Rachel, I want you to look at your part in this plan for capturing and saving the Rectangle. Your voice is a power. I have had many ideas lately. Here is one of them. You could organize among the girls a musical institute. Give them the benefit of your training. There are some splendid voices in the rough there. Did anyone ever hear such singing as that yesterday by those women? Rachel, what a beautiful opportunity! You shall have the best that money can buy in the way of musical equipment."

Before Virginia had ceased speaking, Rachel's face was transfigured with the thought of her life work. It flowed into her heart and mind like a flood, and the torrent of her feeling overflowed in tears that could not be restrained. It was what she had dreamed of doing herself. It was also in keeping with a right use of her talent.

Both young women, in the excitement of their enthusiasm, wept openly.

"Yes, I will gladly put my life into that kind of service!" exclaimed Rachel. "I do believe that Jesus would have me use my life this way. Virginia, what miracles we can accomplish for humanity if we have such a lever as consecrated money with which to move things!"

When Rollin joined them for a brief discussion of their future plans, Rachel studied him with interest. The dissolute look was gone from his face. Eyes that had been listless were now alive with expectancy. Already there seemed to be a firming up of his jawline. His manner toward her was warm, yet somehow cautious, even hesitant. After Rollin left, Rachel and Virginia began to talk of other things.

"By the way, what has become of Jasper Chase?" Virginia asked. When Rachel blushed Virginia added with a smile, "Is he going to put you into his new book, Rachel?"

Rachel replied with the frankness that had always existed between the two friends. "Jasper proposed to me several weeks ago after one of the tent meetings. I thought that I loved him as he said he loved me, but when he spoke, my heart felt repelled. Somehow his timing was all wrong. I'm afraid my rejection is the reason we haven't seen him lately."

"I am glad for you," said Virginia quietly.

"Why?" asked Rachel, a little startled.

"Because I never thought Jasper Chase was right for you. He's too cold. And I don't like to judge him, but I questioned his sincerity in taking the pledge at the church with the rest."

Rachel looked at Virginia thoughtfully.

"He touched my emotions and I admired his skill as a writer. I thought at times that I cared a good deal for him. I think, perhaps, if he had spoken to me at any other time than the one he chose, I could easily have persuaded myself that I loved him. But not now."

Rachel paused suddenly, aware again at the amazing changes taking place in both of them. Where would the Lord lead them next?

14

Virginia stared at her younger brother with intense interest. The change in Rollin delighted her, astounded her. Yet she was puzzled about something. There was an undercurrent of feeling between Rollin and Rachel she did not understand.

"Did you ever know anyone so willing to give her whole life to people as Rachel is going to do?" she asked. "Rachel plans to give music lessons in the city in order to make a living, and then give the Rectangle people the benefit of her culture and her voice."

"It is certainly a good example of self-sacrifice," replied Rollin a little stiffly.

Virginia looked at him quizzically.

"But don't you think it is a very unusual example? Can you imagine"—here Virginia named half-a-dozen famous opera singers—"doing anything of this sort?"

"No, I can't," Rollin answered briefly.

"Then why do you treat her in such a distant manner? I think she is annoyed by it. You two used to be on such good terms."

"Virginia, don't you know how I really feel?" Rollin asked in a sudden agitation.

Virginia looked bewildered then slowly a look of understanding crept over her face.

"I have never loved anyone but Rachel Winslow." Rollin forced himself to speak calmly. "That day she was here when you talked about her refusal to join the concert company, I asked her to be my wife. She turned me down, as I knew she would. And she gave as her reason the fact that I had no purpose in life, which was true. Now that I have a purpose, now that I am a new man, don't you see, Virginia, how impossible it is for me to say anything? I owe my very conversion to Rachel's singing. And yet during that night while she sang I can honestly say I never thought of her voice except as God's message to me. Suddenly all my love for her was redirected into a new and wonderful love for God." Rollin paused, then went on with more emotion.

"I am still in love with Rachel, Virginia. But I do not think she could ever love me." He looked his sister in the face with a sad smile.

Virginia did not agree with her brother's conclusion at all, but she knew in her heart that this was a matter that had to wait. As a new believer Rollin had to prove himself in his efforts to open the hearts of his club friends to the love of Jesus. She wondered how long it would take for God to transform a man from a weakling into a person of strength and courage.

The next day Virginia went down to the *News* office to see Edward Norman and arrange the details of her part in the establishment of the paper on its new foundation. Mr. Maxwell was present at this conference, and the three agreed that, whatever Jesus might do in detail as editor of a daily paper, He would be guided by the same general principles that directed His conduct as the Savior of the world.

"I have tried to put down here in specific form some of these things," said Edward Norman. As he read from a paper lying on his desk, Henry Maxwell was reminded again of his own effort to put into written form his own conception of Jesus's probable action and also of Milton Wright's attempt to do this in his business.

The list was headed by the title "What would Jesus do as Edward Norman, editor of a daily newspaper in Raymond?"

1. He would never allow a sentence or a picture in His paper that could be called bad or coarse or vulgar in any way.

2. He would probably conduct the political part of the paper from the standpoint of nonpartisan patriotism, always looking upon all political questions in the light of their relation to the Kingdom of God, and advocating measures from the standpoint of their relation to the welfare of the people. He would consider them on the basis of, "What is right?" never from the basis of, "What is for the best interest of this or that party?" In other words, He would treat all political questions as He would treat every other subject––from the standpoint of the advancement of the Kingdom of God on earth.

Edward Norman looked up from the reading for a moment. "You understand that this is my opinion of Jesus's probable action on political matters in a daily paper. I am not passing judgment on the other newspapermen who might have a different conception from mine of Jesus's action. I am simply trying to answer honestly, 'What would Jesus do as Edward Norman?'"

3. The primary aim of a daily paper conducted by Jesus would be to do the will of God. That is, His main purpose in carrying on a newspaper would not be to make money or gain political influence, but His first and ruling purpose would be to so conduct His paper that it would be evident to all His subscribers that He was trying to seek first the Kingdom of God by means of His paper. This purpose would be as distinct and unquestioned as the purpose of a minister or a missionary doing Christian work.

4. No questionable advertisements would be accepted.

5. Jesus would expect my relationship with all employees on the paper to be of the most loving character.

"Once you introduce the element of personal love into a business like this," said Norman, again looking up, "and reduce the selfish principle of doing it for the sake of personal profits to a man or company, I think you will find developing a completely new attitude between editors, reporters, pressmen and all who contribute anything to the life of the paper."

6. As editor of a daily paper today, Jesus would give space to the work of the Christian world. He would devote a page possibly to the facts of reform, of sociological problems, of church work, and similar movements.

7. He would fight crime and corruption and the liquor interests as an enemy of the human race and an unwelcome part of our present civilization. He would do this regardless of public sentiment in the matter, always regardless of its effect on His subscription list.

8. Jesus would not issue a Sunday edition.

9. He would print the news of the world that people ought to know. This would not include the detailed accounts of brutal prize fights, or crimes, or scandals in private families, or any other events that degrade mankind. This does not mean that negative news would be excluded, since people need to know both the good and bad news of our life today.

10. Whatever needs might arise as the paper developed along its definite plan, the main principle that guided it would always be the establishment of the Kingdom of God in the world. This large general principle would necessarily shape all the details.

Edward Norman finished reading the plan. He was very thoughtful.

"This is only a rough outline. I have a hundred ideas for making the paper more effective that I have not thought out fully as yet. I have talked it over with other newspapermen. Some of them say I will have a weak, namby-pamby Sunday school sheet. Why do men, when they want to characterize something as particularly feeble, always use Sunday school as a comparison, when they ought to know that the Sunday school program is—or should be—one of the strongest, most powerful influences in shaping the character of men and of nations? But the paper will not necessarily be weak because it is good. Good things are more powerful than bad.

"The big question before me is how much support will I have from the Christian people of Raymond. There are over twenty thousand church members in this city. If half of them will stand by the *News*, its life is assured. What do you think, Henry? Is there probability of such support?"

"I don't know enough about it to give an intelligent answer. I believe in the paper with all my heart. If it lives a year, there is no telling what it will do. The important thing will be to put into it all the elements of Christian strength, intelligence, and sense; to command respect for freedom from bigotry, fanaticism, narrowness and anything else that is contrary to the Spirit of Jesus. Such a paper will call for the best that human thought and action are capable of giving. The greatest minds in the world would have their powers taxed to the utmost to issue a Christian daily."

"Yes," Edward Norman said humbly, "I shall make a great many mistakes, no doubt. I need a great deal of wisdom."

"I think we are beginning to understand," said Virginia, "the meaning of that command, 'Grow in the grace and knowledge of our Lord and Savior Jesus Christ.' I am sure I do not know all that He would do in detail, but as I grow in grace, I'm getting to know Him better."

"That is very true," said Henry Maxwell. "I am beginning to understand that I cannot interpret the probable action of Jesus until I know His Spirit better. The greatest question in all of human life is summed up when we ask, 'What would Jesus do?', if, as we ask it, we also try to answer it from a growth in knowledge of Jesus Himself. We must know Jesus before we can imitate Him.'

When the arrangements had been made between Virginia and Edward Norman, he found himself in the possession of the sum of a half-million dollars to use for the establishment of a Christian daily paper. When Virginia and Maxwell had gone, Norman closed his door and asked like a child for help from his all-powerful Father. All through his prayer as he knelt before his desk ran the promise: "If any man lack wisdom let him ask of God who giveth to all men liberally and upbraideth not, and it shall be given him."

Two months went by. They were full of action and of results in the city of Raymond, and especially in the First Church. In spite of the approaching heat of the summer season, the after-meeting of the disciples who had made the pledge to do as Jesus would do continued with enthusiasm and power. Mr. Gray had finished his work at the Rectangle, and though an outward observer going through the place might not have seen any difference in the old conditions, there was an actual change in hundreds of lives.

Still, the saloon, vice dens, and gambling houses continued to overflow their vileness into the lives of fresh victims to take the place of those rescued by the evangelist. The devil recruited his ranks very fast.

Henry Maxwell did not go abroad. Instead, he took the money he had been saving for the trip and quietly arranged a summer vacation for a family of six living down in the Rectangle who had never gone outside of their tenement area. The pastor of the First Church had quite an experience with this family making the arrangements. He went down into the Rectangle one hot day and helped the family to the railroad station, then went with them to a beautiful spot on the Maine coast where, in the home of a Christian woman, the bewildered city tenants breathed the cool salt air and felt blow about them the pine-scented fragrance of a Maine forest.

Of the four children one was crippled, and the baby was sickly. During the journey the father held the baby in his arms. Later he confessed to Maxwell that he had been out of work for such a long time, that he had several times considered suicide. When Maxwell started back to Raymond after seeing the family settled, to his consternation the man held his hand and, choked with gratitude, wept openly. The mother, a wearied, worn-out woman, had lost three children the year before from a fever scourge in the Rectangle. She sat by the train window all throughout the journey and drank in the delights of sea, sky, and field. It all seemed a miracle to her.

As Henry Maxwell rode back into Raymond at the end of that week, he felt the scorching, sickening heat all the more because of his little taste of the ocean breezes. But he thanked God for the joy he had witnessed, and for learning about this special kind of sacrifice. Never before had he denied himself his regular summer trip away from the heat of Raymond, whether he felt in any great need of rest or not.

"It is a fact," he said, in reply to several inquiries from parishioners, "that I do not feel in need of a vacation this year. I am very well and prefer to stay here." It was with a feeling of relief that he succeeded in concealing from everyone but his wife what he had done with this other family. He was convinced that actions of this sort should be handled without publicity, which would usually bring the approval of others.

So the summer came on, and First Church was still swayed by the power of the Holy Spirit. Maxwell marveled at the continuance of His stay. He knew very well that from the beginning nothing but the Spirit's presence had kept the church from being torn asunder by the remarkable testing it had received of its discipleship. Many members among those who had not taken the pledge regarded the whole movement as Mrs. Winslow did—in the nature of a fanatical interpretation of Christian duty—and looked for a return to the old normal condition. Meanwhile, the pastor went his way that summer doing his parish work in great joy, keeping up his meetings with the railroad men as he had promised Alexander Powers, and daily growing into a better knowledge of the Master.

Early one afternoon in August, after a day of refreshing coolness following a long period of heat, Jasper Chase walked to the window of his room in the apartment house on the avenue and looked out.

On his desk lay a pile of manuscripts. Since that evening when he had been rebuffed by Rachel Winslow he had not seen her. His singularly sensitive nature, sensitive to the point of irritability when he was thwarted, seemed to have thrust him into an isolation intensified by his habits as an author.

All through the heat of the summer he had been writing. His book was nearly done now. He had thrown himself into its construction with a feverish strength that threatened at any moment to desert him and leave him helpless. He had not forgotten his pledge made with the other church members at the First Church. It kept intruding on his thoughts: Would Jesus do this? Would He write this story?

It was a society novel written in a style that had proved popular. It had no purpose except to amuse. Its moral teaching was not bad, but neither was it Christian in any positive way.

Jasper Chase knew that such a story would probably sell. He was conscious of powers in his style that the social world petted and admired. Yet he had to admit to himself that Jesus would never write such a book. The question obtruded on him at the most inopportune times, making him downright irascible.

The standard of Jesus as an author was too ideal. Of course Jesus would use His powers to produce something useful, or helpful, or with purpose. For what reason was he, Jasper Chase, writing this novel? Why, what nearly every writer wrote for—money and fame as an author. He was not poor, and so had no great temptation to write for money. But he was urged on by his desire for fame as much as anything. He must write this kind of matter.

But what would Jesus do? The question plagued him even more than Rachel's refusal. Was he going to break his promise? Did the promise mean much, after all?

As Jasper Chase looked out his window, Rollin Page emerged from the clubhouse just opposite. Jasper noted his handsome face and trim figure as he started down the street. He went back to his desk for a moment and then returned to the window. Rollin was walking down the block and Rachel Winslow was now beside him. Rollin must have overtaken her.

Jasper watched the two figures until they disappeared. Then he turned to his desk and began to write. When he had finished the last page of the last chapter of his book it was nearly dark. What would Jesus do? Jasper had finally answered the question by denying his Lord. It grew darker in his room. He had deliberately chosen his course, urged on by his disappointment and loss.

15

When Rollin left his club and started down the street that afternoon he had come suddenly and accidentally upon Rachel Winslow. His heart had leaped at the sight of her slim graceful figure. He walked along by her now, his spirit rejoicing.

"I have just been to see Virginia," said Rachel. "She tells me the arrangements are nearly completed for the purchase of the Rectangle property."

"Yes. It was slow going through the court. Did Virginia show you all the plans and specifications for the buildings?"

We looked over a good many. It is astonishing to me how many ideas Virginia has."

"Virginia knows more about church procedure in America than a good many professional slum workers. She has been spending nearly all summer in getting information." Rollin was beginning to feel more at ease as they talked about this project. It was safe common ground.

"What have you been doing all summer?" Rachel asked suddenly. "I have not seen much of you." Then her face warmed slightly, as if she might have implied more interest in Rollin than she felt.

"I've been busy," replied Rollin briefly.

"Tell me something about it," persisted Rachel. "You say so little. Have I a right to ask?"

"Yes, certainly," he replied with a grateful smile. "I am not certain I can tell you much. I have been trying to find some way to reach the men I once knew—"

He stopped suddenly as if he were almost afraid to go on. Yet he was encouraged by the interest on Rachel's face.

"I made the pledge to do as I believe Jesus would do. Then I asked myself, 'Where would I be of any use to Him?' Where else but with my old friends?"

"That is what I do not understand. What can you do with the clubmen?"

"Did it ever occur to you that of all the neglected beings in our social system, none are quite so completely left alone as the fast young men who fill the clubs and waste their time and money as I used to do?" replied Rollin. "The churches do show concern for the poor miserable creatures like those in the Rectangle. They make some effort to reach the working men. They send money and missionaries to foreign lands. But there are no Christian efforts for reaching the fashionable, dissipate young men around town, the clubmen.

"And yet no class of people needs it more. I said to myself: 'I know these men, their good and bad qualities. I have been one of them. I am not fitted to reach the Rectangle people; they would ridicule me. But I think I could possibly help some of my friends.' So that is what I have been trying to do." He paused. "It has also been my cross."

Rollin's voice was so low on the last sentence that Rachel barely heard him. She hesitated to ask what his methods were. Her interest in his plans was larger than mere curiosity. Rollin Page was so different now from the dissipated young man who had asked her to be his wife that she could not help thinking of him as if he were an entirely new acquaintance.

They had turned up the street to Rachel's home. It was the same street where Rollin had asked Rachel why she could not love him. They were both stricken with a sudden shyness as they went on.

"In your work with the clubmen, with your old acquaintances, what sort of reception do they give you? How do you approach them? What do they say?" she finally asked.

"It depends on the man. A good many of them think I am a crank. I try to be wise. Some of the men have responded. Only a few nights ago a dozen of us became honestly and earnestly engaged in a conversation over religious questions. I have had the great joy of seeing several of the men question their own morality. A few have started going to church. I'm too new a Christian to be a good evangelist, so I am feeling my way along. One thing I have found out. The men are not avoiding me. I think that is a good sign. Another thing, I have interested some of them in the Rectangle work. And in addition to all the rest, I have found a way to steer several young fellows away from the clutches of gamblers."

Rollin spoke with enthusiasm. His face was transformed by his interest in the subject that had now become a part of his real life. Rachel again noted the vitality of his speech. Underneath it all was a new and deep seriousness.

"Do you remember I reproached you once for not having any purpose worth living for?" she asked. "I want to say that I honor you now for your courage and your obedience to the promise you have made."

They walked along in silence. Finally, Rollin said uncertainly, "I thank you. It has been worth more to me than I can tell you to hear you say that." He looked into her face for one moment. She read his love for her in that look.

When they separated, Rachel went into the house, and sitting down in her room said to herself, "I am beginning to know what it means to be loved by a real man."

She rose and walked back and forth. Somehow a glad, new joy had come to her. And she also realized that if she were beginning to love Rollin Page, it was the Christian man she had begun to love. The other person never would have moved her to this change.

And Rollin, as he walked to his home, treasured a hope that had been a stranger to him since Rachel said no that day on the street. In that hope he went on with his work in renewed enthusiasm.

The summer had gone and Raymond was once more facing the rigor of her winter season. Virginia had been able to accomplish a part of her plan for "capturing the Rectangle," as she called it. But building of houses in the areas and transforming its bleak, bare aspect into an attractive park—all of which was included in her plan—was too large a work to be completed that fall after she had secured the property.

Henry Maxwell was impressed, however, by how much had been done in a short time. Yet as he walked through the Rectangle one day, he could not avoid the question of the continual degradation of life there. How much had been done for this area after all? Of course, he said to himself, the redemptive work begun and carried on by the Holy Spirit in the tent meetings had had its effect on the life of all of Raymond. But as he walked past saloon after saloon and noted the crowds going in and coming out of them; as he saw the wretched dens—as many as ever, apparently; as he caught the brutality and squalor and open misery and degradation on countless faces of men and women and children, he sickened at the sight.

He found himself asking how much cleansing a million dollars poured into this cesspool could accomplish. What could even such unselfish Christian discipleship as Virginia's and Rachel's do to lesson the stream of vice, so long as the great spring of vice and crime flowed as deep and strong as ever? Was it not a practical waste of beautiful lives for these young women to throw themselves into this earthly hell, when for every soul rescued by their sacrifice the saloon made two more that needed rescue?

He could not escape the question. It was the same that Virginia had put to Rachel in her statement that, in her opinion, nothing really permanent would ever be done until the saloon was taken out of the Rectangle. Henry Maxwell went back to his parish work that afternoon with added convictions on the license business.

But if the saloon was a factor in the life of Raymond, no less was First Church and its little company of disciples who had pledged to do as Jesus would do. Henry Maxwell, standing at the very center of the movement, was not in a position to judge its power as someone from the outside might have done. But Raymond itself felt the touch in many ways, not knowing all the reasons for the change.

16

The winter had passed and the year was ended—the year which Henry Maxwell had fixed as the time during which the pledge should be kept to do as Jesus would do. The year had made history so quickly that few people were able to grasp its significance. And the anniversary Sunday itself, which marked the completion of a whole year of such discipleship, was characterized by such revelations and confessions that the immediate actors in the events themselves could not understand the value of what had been done, or the relationship of their trial to the rest of the churches and cities in the country.

It happened that the week before the anniversary Sunday, the Reverend Calvin Bruce, DD, of the Nazareth Avenue Church in Chicago, was in Raymond visiting some friends and, incidentally, to see his old seminary classmate, Henry Maxwell. He was present at First Church and was an exceedingly attentive and interested spectator. His account of events in Raymond, and especially of that Sunday, was sent in the form of a letter to his friend, the Reverend Philip A. Caxton:

My dear Caxton:

It is late Sunday night, but I am so intensely awake and so overflowing with what I have seen and heard that I feel driven to write you some account of the situation in Raymond, as it came to a climax today. So this is my reason for writing so extended a letter at this time.

You remember Henry Maxwell when we were in seminary. I think you said, the last time I visited you in New York, that you had not seen him since we graduated. He was a refined, scholarly fellow, you remember, and when he was called to the first Church of Raymond within a year after leaving the seminary, I said to my wife, "Raymond has made a good choice. Maxwell will satisfy them as a sermonizer."

He has been here eleven years, and I understand that up to a year ago he had performed a routine sort of ministry, giving good satisfaction and drawing a good congregation. His church was considered the largest and wealthiest in Raymond. All the best people attended it, and most of them belonged. The quartet choir was famous for its music, especially for its soprano, Rachel Winslow, of whom I shall have more to say: and on the whole, as I understand the facts, Maxwell was in a comfortable berth, with a very good salary, pleasant surroundings, not a very exciting parish of refined rich, respectable people, the kind of church nearly all young men of the seminary looked forward to as very desirable.

But a year ago today, Maxwell came into this church on Sunday morning, and at the close of the service made the astounding proposition that the members of his church volunteer for a year not to do anything without first asking the question, "What would Jesus do?" and, after answering it, to do what in their honest judgment He would do, regardless of what the result might be to them.

The effect of this proposition, as it has been met and obeyed by a number of the members of the church, has been so remarkable that, as you know, the attention of the whole country has been directed to the movement. I call it a movement because, from the action taken today, it seems probable that what has been tried here will reach out into the other churches and cause revolution in methods, but more especially give a new definition to Christian discipleship.

In the first place, Maxwell tells me he was astonished at the response to his proposition. Some of the most prominent members in the church made the promise to do as Jesus would. Among them were Edward Norman, the editor of the *Daily News*, which has since made such a sensation in the newspaper world; Milton Wright, one of the leading merchants in Raymond; Alexander Powers, whose action in the matter of railroads against the interstate commerce laws created such a stir about a year ago; Virginia Page, one of Raymond's leading society heiresses who has lately dedicated her entire fortune, as I understand, to Norman's paper and the work of reform in the slum district known as the Rectangle; and Rachel Winslow, whose reputation as a singer is now national, but who had decided to devote her talent to volunteer work among the girls and women who make up a large part of the city's worst and most abandoned population.

In addition to these well-known people, a gradually increasing number of Christians from the First Church, and lately from other churches in Raymond, have taken up the challenge. A large proportion of these volunteers who pledge themselves to do as Jesus would come from the Endeavor Societies. The young people say that they have already embodied in their society pledge the same principles in the words: "I promise Him that I will strive to do whatever He would have me do." This is not exactly what is included in Maxwell's proposition, which is that the disciples shall try to do what Jesus would probably do in the disciple's place. But the result of an honest obedience to either pledge, he claims, will be virtually the same.

I am sure the first question you will ask is, What has been the result of this attempt? What has it accomplished, or how has it changed in any way the regular course of the church or community?

You already know something from reports of Raymond that have gone over the country what the results have been. But one needs to come here and learn something of the changes in individual lives, and especially the change in the church life, to realize all that is meant by this following of Jesus's steps so literally. To tell all would be to write a long story or series of stories. I am not in a position to do that, but I can give you some idea, perhaps, of what has been done as told me by friends and by Maxwell himself.

The result of the pledge upon the First Church has been twofold. It has brought about a spirit of Christian fellowship which Maxwell tells me never before existed, and which now impresses him as being very nearly what the Christian fellowship of the apostolic churches must have been; and it has divided the church into two distinct groups of members.

Those who have not taken the pledge regard the others as foolishly literal in their attempts to imitate the example of Jesus. Some of them have withdrawn from the church and no longer attend, or they have removed their membership entirely to other churches. Some are an element of internal strife, and I have heard rumors of an attempt on their part to force Maxwell's resignation. I do not know that this element is very strong in the church. It has been held in check by a wonderful continuance of spiritual power, which dates from the first Sunday the pledge was taken a year ago, and also by the fact that so many of the most prominent members had been identified with the movement.

The effect on Maxwell is marked. I heard him preach at our State Association four years ago. He impressed me at the time as having considerable power in dramatic delivery, of which he himself was somewhat conscious. His sermon was well-written and abounded in what the seminary students used to call "fine passages." The effect of it was what an average congregation would call pleasing.

This morning I heard Maxwell preach again for the first time since then. I shall speak of that farther on. He is not the same man. He gives me the impression of one who has passed through an internal revolution. He tells me this revolution is simply a new definition of Christian discipleship. He certainly has changed many of his old habits and many of his old views. His attitude on the saloon question is radically opposite to the one he entertained a year ago.

And in the entire thought of his ministry, his pulpit and parish work, I find he has made a complete change. So far as I can understand, the idea that is moving him on now is the idea that the Christianity of our times must represent a more literal imitation of Jesus, and especially in the element of sacrifice. He quoted to me in the course of our conversation the verses in Peter: "For even hereunto were ye called, because Christ also suffered for us, leaving us an example, that ye should follow his steps." He seems filled with the conviction that what our churches need today more than anything else is this factor of joyful sacrifice for Jesus in some form.

I do not know as I agree with him altogether; but, my dear Caxton, it is certainly astonishing to note the results of these ideas as they have impressed themselves upon this city and this church.

You ask about the results on the individuals who have made this pledge and honestly tried to be true to it. Those results are, as I have said, a part of individual history and cannot be told in detail. Some of them I can give you so that you may see that this form of discipleship is not merely sentiment or fine posing for effect.

For instance, take the case of Alexander Powers, who was superintendent of the machine shops of the L. and T.R.R. here. When he acted upon the evidence which incriminated the railroad, he lost his position and, more than that, I learn from my friends here, his family and social relations have become so estranged that the family no longer appears in public. They have dropped out of the social circle where once they were so prominent.

By the way, Caxton, I understand in this connection that the Commission, for one reason or another, postponed action on this case and it is now rumored that the L. and T.R.R. will pass into a receiver's hands very soon. The president of the railroad, who, according to the evidence submitted by Powers, was the principal offender, has resigned, and complications which have since arisen point to the receivership.

Meanwhile, the superintendent has gone back to his old work as a telegraph operator. I met him at the church yesterday. He impressed me as a man who had, like Maxwell, gone through a crisis in character. I could not help thinking of him as being good material for the church of the first century when the disciples had all things in common.

Or take the case of Edward Norman, editor of the *Daily News*. He risked his entire fortune in obedience to what he believed was Jesus's action and revolutionized his entire conduct of the paper at the risk of failure. I am sending you a copy of yesterday's paper. I want you to read it carefully. To my mind it is one of the most interesting and remarkable papers ever printed in the United States. It is open to criticism, but what could any mere man attempt in this line that would be free from criticism? Taken all in all, it is so far above the ordinary conception of a daily paper that I am amazed at the result. He tells me that the paper is beginning to be read more and more by the Christian people of the city. He is very confident of its final success.

Read his editorial on the money question, also the one on the coming election in Raymond, when the question of license will again be an issue. Both articles are outstanding. He says he never begins an editorial, or in fact, any part of his newspaper work, without first asking, "What would Jesus do?" The result is certainly apparent.

Then, there is Milton Wright, the merchant. He has, I am told, so revolutionized his business that no man is more beloved today in Raymond. His own clerks and employees have affection for him that is very touching. During the winter, while he was lying dangerously ill at his home, scores of clerks volunteered to watch or help in any possible way, and his return to his store was greeted with marked demonstrations.

All this has been brought about by the element of personal love introduced into the business. This love is not mere words, but the business itself is carried on under a system of cooperation that is not a patronizing recognition of inferiors but a real sharing in the whole business. Other men on the street look upon Milton Wright as odd. It is a fact, however, that while he has lost heavily in some directions, he has increased his business and is today respected and honored as one of the best and most successful merchants in Raymond.

And there is Rachel Winslow. She has chosen to give her great talent to the poor of the city. Her plans include a musical institute where choruses and classes in vocal music shall be a feature. She is enthusiastic over her life work. In connection with her friend, Virginia Page, she had planned a course in music which, if carried out, will certainly do much to lift up the lives of the people down there.

I am not too old, dear Caxton, to be interested in the romantic side of much that has also been tragic here in Raymond, and I must tell you that it is well understood here that Miss Winslow expects to be married this spring to a brother of Miss Page, who was once a society leader and clubman, and who was converted in a tent where his wife-to-be took an active part in the service. I don't know all the details of this romance, but I can imagine there is a story wrapped up in it, and it would make interesting reading if we only knew it all.

These are only a few illustrations of results in individual lives owing to obedience to the pledge. I meant to have spoken to President Marsh of Lincoln College. He is a graduate of my alma mater, and I knew him slightly when I was in my senior year. He has taken an active part in the recent municipal campaign, and his influence in the city is regarded as a very large factor in the coming election. He impressed me, as did all the other disciples in this movement, as having fought out some hard questions and as having taken up some real burdens that have caused and still do cause that suffering of which Henry Maxwell speaks, a suffering that does not eliminate but does appear to intensify a positive and practical joy.

But I am prolonging this letter, possibly to your weariness. I am unable to avoid the feeling of fascination which my entire stay here has increased. I want to tell you something of the meeting in First Church today.

As I said, I heard Maxwell preach. At his earnest request I had preached for him the Sunday before, and this was the first time I had heard him since the Association meeting four years ago. His sermon this morning was as different from his sermon then as if it had been thought out and preached by someone living on another planet. I was profoundly touched. I believe I actually shed tears once. Others in the congregation were moved like myself.

His text was, "What Is That to Thee? Follow Thou Me." It was a most unusually impressive appeal to the Christians of Raymond to obey Jesus's teachings and follow in His steps regardless of what others might do. I cannot give you even the plan of the sermon. It would take too long. At the close of the service, there was the usual after-meeting that has become a regular feature of the First Church. Into this meeting come all those who have made the pledge to do as Jesus would do, and this time is spent in mutual fellowship, confession, questions as to what Jesus would do in special cases, and prayer that the one great guide of every disciple's conduct may be the Holy Spirit.

Maxwell asked me to come into this meeting. Nothing in all my ministerial life, Caxton, has so moved me as that experience. I have never felt the Spirit's presence so powerfully. It was a meeting of reminiscences and of the most loving fellowship. I was irresistibly driven in thought back to the first years of Christianity. There was something about all this that was apostolic in its simplicity and Christlikeness.

I asked questions. One that seemed to arouse more interest than any other was in regard to the extent of the Christian disciple's sacrifice of personal property. Maxwell tells me that, so far, no one has interpreted the Spirit of Jesus in such a way as to abandon his earthly possessions, give away all his wealth, or in any literal way imitate the Christians of the order, for example, of St. Francis of Assisi.

It was the unanimous consent, however, that if any disciple should feel that Jesus in his own particular case would do that, there could be only one answer to the question. Maxwell admitted that he was still, to a certain degree, uncertain as to Jesus's probable action when it came to the details of household living, the possession of wealth, the holding of certain luxuries. It is evident, however, that many of these disciples have repeatedly carried their obedience to Jesus to the extreme limit, regardless of financial loss. There is no lack of courage or consistency at this point.

It is also true that some of the businessmen who took the pledge have lost large sums of money in this imitation of Jesus, and many have, like Alexander Powers, lost valuable positions. In connection with these cases, it is pleasant to record that many who have suffered in this way have at once been helped financially by those who still have means. In this respect I think it is true that these disciples have all things in common. Certainly such scenes as I witnessed at the First Church at that after-service this morning I never saw in my church or any other. I never dreamed that such Christian fellowship could exist in this day and age. I am almost incredulous as to the witness of my own senses.

But now, dear friend, I come to the real cause of the letter, the real heart of the whole question as the First Church of Raymond has forced it upon me. Before the meeting closed today, steps were taken to secure the cooperation of all other Christian disciples in this country. I think Maxwell took this step after long deliberation. He said as much to me one day when we were discussing the effect of this movement upon the church in general.

"Why," he said, "suppose that the church membership generally in this country made this pledge and lived up to it! What a revolution it would cause in Christendom! And why not? Is it any more than the disciple ought to do? Has he followed Jesus unless he is willing to do this? Is the test of discipleship any less today than it was in Jesus's time?"

179

I do not know all that preceded or followed Maxwell's thought of what ought to be done outside Raymond, but the idea crystallized today in a plan to secure the fellowship of all the Christians in America. The churches, through their pastors, will be asked to form disciple gatherings like the one in the First Church. Volunteers will be called for in the great body of church members in the United States who will promise to do as Jesus would do. Surely, if First Church could work such changes in society and its surroundings, the church in general by combining such fellowship, not of creed but of conduct, ought to stir the entire nation to a higher life and a new conception of Christianity.

This is a grand idea, Caxton, but right here is where I find myself hesitating. I do not deny that the Christian disciple ought to follow Christ's steps as closely as these here in Raymond have tried to do. But I cannot avoid asking what the result will be if I ask my church in Chicago to do it.

I am writing this after feeling the solemn profound touch of the Spirit's presence, and I confess to you, old friend, that I cannot call up in my church a dozen prominent business or professional men who would make this trial at the risk of all that they hold dear. Can you do any better in your church? What are we to say? That the church would not respond to the call *Come and suffer*? Is our standard of Christian discipleship a wrong one, or are we possibly deceiving ourselves and would be agreeably surprised if we once asked our people to take such a pledge faithfully?

The actual results of the pledge as obeyed here in Raymond are enough to make any pastor tremble and, at the same time, long with yearning that they might occur in his own parish. Never have I seen a church so signally blessed by the Spirit as this one, but—am I myself ready to take this pledge? I ask the question honestly and I dread to face an honest answer. I know well enough that I would have to change very much in my own life if I undertook to follow His steps so closely.

I have called myself a Christian for many years. For the past ten years I have enjoyed a life that has had comparatively little sacrifice in it. I am living at a long distance from municipal problems and the life of the poor, the degraded and the abandoned. What would obedience to this pledge demand of me? I hesitate to answer. My church is wealthy, full of well-to-do, satisfied people. The standard of their discipleship is, I predict, not of a nature to respond to a call to suffering or personal loss. I say "I predict," but I may be mistaken. I may have erred in not stirring their deeper life.

Caxton, my friend, I have spoken my inmost thought to you. Shall I go back to my people next Sunday and stand up before them in my large city church and say, "Let us follow Jesus more closely. Let us walk in His steps where it will cost us something more than it is costing now. Let us pledge not to do anything without first asking, 'What would Jesus do?'" If I should go before them with that message, it would be strange and startling to them. But why should it be?

The Reverend Calvin Bruce, DD, of the Nazareth Avenue Church, Chicago, let his pen fall on the paper. He had come to the central issue, and his question, he felt sure, was the question of many a man in the ministry and in the church. He went to his window and opened it. He was oppressed with the weight of his convictions, and he felt almost suffocated with the air of the room. He wanted to see the stars and feel the breath of the world.

The night was very still. The clock in First Church was just striking midnight. As it finished, a clear, strong voice down in the direction of the Rectangle came floating up to him as if borne on radiant pinions.

It was the voice of one of Gray's old converts, a night watchman at the packinghouse, who sometimes solaced his lonesome hours by a verse or two from some familiar hymn.

> Must Jesus bear the cross alone,
> And all the world go free?
> No! There's a cross for everyone,
> And there's a cross for me.

The Reverend Calvin Bruce turned away from the window and, after a little hesitation, he knelt. "What would Jesus do?" That was the burden of his prayer. Never had he yielded himself so completely to the Spirit's searching, revealing of Jesus.

He was on his knees a long time. Then he retired and slept fitfully, with many awakenings. He rose before it was clear dawn and threw open his window again. As the light in the east grew stronger, he repeated to himself, "What would Jesus do? Shall I follow His steps?"

The sun rose and flooded the city with its light. When shall the dawn of a new discipleship usher in the conquering triumph of a closer walk with Jesus? When shall Christendom tread more closely the path He made?

> It is the way the Master trod,
> Shall not the servant tread it still?

With this question throbbing through his whole being, the Reverend Calvin Bruce took the train back to Chicago, little realizing that the greatest crisis of his Christian ministry was about to break irresistibly upon him.

17

The Saturday matinee at the Auditorium in Chicago was just over; and the crowd was struggling out the aisles to the street.

Two girls stepped out of the crowd toward one of the carriages. The older one had entered and taken her seat, and the attendant was still holding the door open for the younger, who stood hesitating on the curb.

"Come, Felicia! What are you waiting for? I shall freeze to death!" called the voice from the carriage.

The girl outside the carriage hastily unpinned a bunch of English violets from her dress and handed them to a small boy who was standing shivering on the edge of the sidewalk. He took them with a look of astonishment and a "Thank ye, lady!" and instantly buried a very grimy face in the bunch of perfume. The girl stepped into the carriage, and in a few moments the coachman was speeding the horses rapidly up one of the boulevards.

"You are always doing some queer thing or other, Felicia," said the older girl.

"Am I? What have I done that is queer now, Rose?" asked Felicia, looking up suddenly and turning her head toward her sister.

"Giving those violets to that boy. He looked as if he needed a good hot supper more than a bunch of violets. It's a wonder you didn't invite him home with us. I shouldn't have been surprised if you had. You are always doing such queer things."

"Would it be queer to invite a boy like that to come to the house and eat a hot supper?" Felicia asked softly, almost as if she were alone.

"Queer isn't just the word, of course," replied Rose indifferently. "It would be what Madame Blanc calls *outré*. Decidedly. Therefore, you will please not invite him, or others like him, to hot suppers because I suggested it. Oh, dear, I'm so tired!"

She yawned as Felicia silently looked out the window.

"The concert was stupid, and the violinist was simply a bore. I don't see how you could sit so still through it all," Rose exclaimed a little impatiently.

"I liked the music," answered Felicia quietly.

"You like anything. I never saw a girl with so little critical taste."

Felicia colored slightly but would not answer. Rose yawned again, then she exclaimed abruptly:

"I'm sick of most everything. I hope the *Shadows of London* will be exciting tonight."

"The *Shadows of Chicago*!" murmured Felicia.

"*Shadows of Chicago, Shadows of London*, who cares what you call the play when it was the sensation of New York for two months. You know we have a box with the Delanos tonight."

Felicia turned toward her sister. Her great brown eyes were impressive and not altogether free from a sparkle of luminous heat.

"And yet we never weep over the real thing on the actual stage of life. What are the shadows of London on the stage to the shadows of London or Chicago as they really exist? Why don't we get excited over the facts as they are?"

"Because the actual people are dirty and disagreeable and it's too much bother, I suppose," replied Rose carelessly. "Felicia, you can never reform the world. What's the use? We're not to blame for the poverty and misery. There have always been rich and poor, and there always will be. We ought to be thankful we're rich."

"Suppose Christ had gone on that principle," replied Felicia with unusual persistence. "Do you remember Dr. Bruce's sermon on that verse a few Sundays ago: 'For ye know the grace of our Lord Jesus Christ, that though he was rich, yet for our sakes he became poor, that ye though his poverty might become rich'?"

"I remember it well enough," said Rose with some petulance. "And didn't Dr. Bruce go on to say that there was no blame attached to people who have wealth if they are kind and give to the needs of the poor? I am sure he himself is pretty comfortably settled. He never gives up his luxuries just because some people go hungry. What good would it do if he did?

"I tell you, Felicia, there will always be poor and rich in spite of all we can do. Ever since Rachel has written about those queer doings in Raymond, you have upset the whole family. People can't live up to such high standards all the time. You see if Rachel doesn't give it up soon. It's a great pity she doesn't come to Chicago and sing in the Auditorium concerts. I heard today that she had received an offer. I'm going to write and urge her to come. I'm just dying to hear her sing."

Felicia looked out the window and was silent. The carriage rolled on past two blocks of magnificent private residences and turned into a wide driveway under a covered passage. The sisters hurried into the house. It was an elegant mansion of gray stone, furnished like a palace, every corner of it warm with the luxury of paintings, sculpture, art, and modern refinement.

The owner of it all, Charles R. Sterling, stood before an open grate fire smoking a cigar. He had made his money in grain speculation and railroad ventures, and was reputed to be worth something over two million. His wife was a sister of Rachel's mother. She had been an invalid for several years. The two girls, Rose and Felicia, were the only children.

Rose was 21, a blonde beauty, educated in a fashionable college, just entering society, and already somewhat cynical and indifferent. A hard young lady to please, her father said about her sometimes playfully, sometimes sternly. Felicia, at 19, had a tropical loveliness somewhat like her cousin Rachel Winslow, with warm, generous impulses just waking into Christian feeling, capable of all sorts of expression: a puzzle to her father, a source of irritation to her mother. There was in Felicia a large unsurveyed territory of thought and action.

"Here's a letter for you, Felicia," said Mr. Sterling.

Felicia took the letter and instantly opened it, saying as she did so, "It's from Rachel."

"Well, what's the latest news from Raymond?" asked Mr. Sterling, taking his cigar out of his mouth and looking at Felicia as he often did—with half-shut eyes, as if he were studying her.

"Rachel says Dr. Bruce has been in Raymond for two Sundays and seems very interested in what has happened at First Church this past year."

"What does Rachel say about herself" asked Rose, who was lying on a couch almost buried in elegant cushions.

"She is still singing at the Rectangle. Since the tent meetings closed, she sings in an old hall until the new buildings that her friend Virginia Page is putting up are completed."

Mr. Sterling relit his cigar as Rose exclaimed, "Rachel is so queer. She might set Chicago wild with her voice if she sang in the Auditorium. And there she goes on, throwing her voice away on people who don't know what they are hearing."

"Rachel won't come here unless she can do it and keep her pledge at the same time," said Felicia after a pause.

"What pledge?" Mr. Sterling asked, and then added vaguely, "Oh, I remember now, that business of letting Jesus run your life." He reflected. "It's rather strange, but Alexander Powers used to be a friend of mine. We learned telegraphy in the same office. Made a great sensation when he resigned and handed over that evidence to the Interstate Commerce Commission. And he's back at his telegraph again. There have been queer doings in Raymond during the past year. I wonder what Dr. Bruce thinks of it on the whole. I must have a talk with him about it."

"He is at home and will preach tomorrow," said Felicia. "Perhaps he will tell us something about it."

There was silence for a minute. Then Felicia said abruptly, "And what if he should propose the same pledge to the Nazareth Avenue Church?"

"What are you talking about?" asked her father a little sharply.

"About Dr. Bruce. I mean, what if he should propose to our church what Mr. Maxwell proposed to his, and ask for volunteers who would pledge themselves to do nothing until asking the question, 'What would Jesus do?'"

"There's no danger of it," said Rose.

"It's a very impractical movement, to my mind," said Mr. Sterling.

"I understand from Rachel's letter that the church in Raymond is going to make an attempt to extend the idea of the pledge to other churches. If it succeeds, it will certainly make great changes in the churches and in people's lives," said Felicia.

"At the moment, all I'm interested in is dinner," said Rose, walking into the dining room. Her father and Felicia followed and the meal proceeded in silence. Mrs. Sterling's meals were served in her room. Mr. Sterling was preoccupied. He ate very little and excused himself early, and although it was Saturday night he remarked as he went out that he would not be home until late because of business matters.

"Don't you think that Father looks disturbed lately?" asked Felicia after he had gone out.

"Oh, I don't know. I hadn't noticed anything unusual," replied Rose. After a silence she said, "Are you going to the play tonight, Felicia? Mrs. Delano will be here at half-past seven. I think you ought to go. She'll feel hurt if you refuse."

"I'll go. I don't care about it, though. I can see shadows enough without going to the play."

"That's a doleful remark for a girl of 19," replied Rose. "But then, you're queer in your ideas anyhow, Felicia. If you're going up to see Mother, tell her I'll run in after the play, if she's still awake."

Felicia went up to see her mother and remained with her until the Delano carriage came. Mrs. Sterling was worried about her husband. She talked incessantly and was irritated by every remark Felicia made. She would not listen to Felicia's attempt to read even a part of Rachel's letter. When Felicia offered to stay with her for the evening, she refused the offer sharply.

Felicia was not happy as she left for the play, but she was familiar with that feeling, except that sometimes she was more unhappy than at other times. Her feeling expressed itself tonight by withdrawal. When the company was seated in the box and the curtain went up, Felicia positioned herself behind the others and remained for the evening by herself. Mrs. Delano, as chaperone for a half-dozen young ladies, understood Felicia well enough to know that she was "a bit strange," as Rose often said, and she made no attempt to draw her out of her corner.

The play was an English melodrama full of startling situations, realistic scenery and unexpected climaxes. There was one scene in the third act that impressed even Rose Sterling. It took place inside one of the slum tenements in the East End of London. Here the scene painter and carpenter had done their utmost to produce an exact copy of a famous court and alley well-known to the poor creatures who made up a part of the outcast London humanity.

The rags, the crowding, the vileness, the broken furniture, the horrible animal existence forced upon creatures made in God's image were shown so skillfully in this scene that more than one elegant woman in the theatre, seated like Rose Sterling in a sumptuous box, surrounded with silk hangings and velvet-covered railing, caught herself shrinking back a little, as if contamination were possible from the nearness of this piece of scenery. It was almost too realistic, and yet it had a horrible fascination for Felicia as she sat there alone, buried back in a cushioned seat and absorbed in thoughts that went far beyond the dialogue on the stage.

From the tenement scene the play shifted to the interior of a nobleman's palace, and something akin to a sigh of relief went up all over the house at the sight of the accustomed luxury of the upper classes. The contrast was startling. It was brought about by a clever piece of staging that allowed only a few minutes to elapse between the slum and the palace scenes.

The dialogue went on, the actors came and went in their various roles, but upon Felicia the play made but one distinct impression. Though the scenes in the slum were only incidents in the story of the play, Felicia found herself living those scenes over and over. She had never philosophized about the causes of human misery. She was not old enough; she had not the temperament. But she felt intensely—and this was not the first time she had felt—the contrast between the upper and lower conditions of human life.

"Come, Felicia, aren't you going home?" said Rose. The play was over, the curtain down, and the people were going noisily out, laughing and gossiping, as if the play were only good diversion.

Felicia aroused herself from her thoughts and quietly went out with the rest. She was never absentminded, but often thought herself into a condition that left her alone in the midst of a crowd.

"Well, what did you think of it?" asked Rose when the sisters had reached home. Rose had considerable respect for Felicia's judgment of a play.

"I thought it a pretty fair picture of real life."

"I mean the acting," said Rose, annoyed.

"The bridge scene was well-acted, especially the woman's part. I thought the man overdid the sentiment a little."

"Did you? I enjoyed that. And wasn't the scene between the two cousins funny when they first learned they were related? But the slum scene was horrible. I think they ought not to show such things in a play. They are too painful."

"They must be painful in real life, too," replied Felicia.

"Yes, but I don't think we should have to pay money to see such things."

"Are you going up to see Mother?" asked Felicia after a pause.

"No," replied Rose from the other room. "I won't trouble her tonight. If you go in, tell her I am too tired to be agreeable."

As Felicia climbed the great staircase and walked down

the upper hall, she could see that the light was still burning in her mother's room. The servant who always waited on Mrs. Sterling was beckoning Felicia to come in.

"Tell Clara to go out," exclaimed Mrs. Sterling as Felicia came up to the bed.

Felicia was surprised, but did as her mother bade her and then inquired how she was feeling.

"Felicia," said her mother. "Can you pray?"

The question was so unlike any her mother had ever asked that Felicia was startled. But she answered, "Why, yes, Mother. Why do you ask such a question?"

"Felicia, I am frightened. Your father—I have had such strange fears about him all day. Something is wrong with him. I want you to pray."

"Now? Here, Mother?"

"Yes. Pray, Felicia."

Felicia reached out and took her mother's hand. It was trembling. Mrs. Sterling had never shown such tenderness for her younger daughter, and her strange demand now was the first real sign of any confidence in Felicia's character.

The girl knelt, still holding her mother's trembling hand, and prayed. It was doubtful if she had ever prayed aloud before. She must have said in her prayer the words that were needed, for when it was silent in the room her mother was weeping softly and her nervous tension was gone.

Felicia stayed there some time. When she was assured that her mother would no longer need her, she rose to go.

"Goodnight, Mother. You must let Clara call me, if you feel bad in the night."

"I feel better now." Then, as Felicia was moving away, Mrs. Sterling said, "Won't you kiss me, Felicia?"

Felicia went back and bent over her mother. The kiss was almost as strange to her as the prayer had been. When Felicia went out of the room, her cheeks were wet with tears. She had not often cried since she was a little girl.

18

Sunday morning at the Sterling mansion was generally very quiet. The girls usually went to church at the eleven o'clock service. Mr. Sterling was not a member but a heavy contributor, and he generally attended with his daughters. This time he did not come down to breakfast, and finally sent word by a servant that he did not feel well enough to go out. So Rose and Felicia drove up to the door of the Nazareth Avenue Church and entered the family pew alone.

When Dr. Bruce walked to the pulpit to open the Bible, as his custom was, those who knew him best did not detect anything unusual in his manner or expression. He proceeded with the service as usual. He was calm and his voice steady and firm. His prayer was the first intimation anyone had of anything new or strange in the service. It is safe to say that the Nazareth Avenue Church had never before heard Dr. Bruce offer such a prayer during the twelve years he had been pastor there.

How would a minister be likely to pray when he had just come out of a revolution in Christian feeling that had completely changed his definition of what was meant by following Jesus? No one in Nazareth Avenue Church had any idea that the Reverend Calvin Bruce, DD, the dignified, cultured, refined doctor of divinity, had within a few days been crying on his knees like a little child, asking for strength and courage and Christlikeness to speak his Sunday message. And yet the prayer was an unconscious involuntary disclosure of the soul's experience such as the Nazareth Avenue people had seldom heard and never before from that pulpit.

In the hush that succeeded the prayer, a distinct wave of spiritual power moved over the congregation. The most careless persons in the church felt it. Felicia, whose sensitive religious nature responded swiftly to every touch of emotion, quivered under the passing of that supernatural Presence; and when she lifted her head and looked up at the minister there was in her eyes a look of intense, eager anticipation.

And she was not alone in her attitude. There was something in the prayer that stirred many a disciple in that church. All over the house, men and women leaned forward; and when Dr. Bruce began to speak of his visit to Raymond, there was a responsiveness from the congregation that he had never before experienced. In his heart he felt a new love for them and at the same time a deep uncertainty in his heart. How many of his fashionable, refined, luxury-loving members would understand the nature of the appeal he was soon to make to them? He was altogether in the dark as to that. Nevertheless, he had been through his desert and had come out of it ready to be tested.

"This morning I would like to tell you about a most exciting work that has been going on in Raymond for the past year," he began. "For the past two weeks I have been somewhat involved in it myself."

Then Dr. Bruce told his people simply but with controlled emotion what had happened at First Church. Felicia listened to every word with strained attention. She sat there by the side of Rose like fire beside snow, although even Rose was as alert as was possible for her to be.

"My friends," he said, "I am going to ask that Nazareth Avenue Church take the same pledge that the Raymond Church has taken. I know what this will mean to you and to me. It will mean the complete change of very many habits. It will mean, possibly, social loss. It will mean, in some cases, loss of money. It will mean sacrifice. It will probably mean what following Jesus meant in the first century, and then it meant suffering, hardship, separation from everything non-Christian. What does following Jesus mean today? The test of discipleship is the same now as then."

Again he paused, and now the result of his announcement was plainly visible in the stir that went over the congregation. He added in a quiet voice that all who volunteered to make the pledge to do as Jesus would do were asked to remain after the morning service.

Immediately he proceeded with his sermon. His text was "Master, I Will Follow Thee Withersoever Thou Goest."

It was a sermon that touched the deep springs of conduct. It was a revelation to the people of the definition their pastor had been learning. It took them back to the first century of

Christianity. Above all, it stirred them below the conventional thought of years as to the meaning and purpose of church membership. It was such a sermon as a man may only be able to preach once in a lifetime, and with enough in it for people to live on all through the rest of their lifetime.

The service closed in a hush that was broken only slowly. People rose here and there, a few at a time. There was a reluctance in the movements of some that was very striking.

Rose, however, walked straight out of the pew, and as she reached the aisle turned her head and beckoned to Felicia. By that time the congregation was rising all over the church.

"I'm going to stay," Felicia said.

Rose had heard her speak in the same manner on other occasions and knew that her resolve could not be changed. Nevertheless, she went back into the pew two or three steps and faced her.

"Felicia," she whispered, a flush of anger on her cheeks, "this is folly. What can you do? What will Father say? Come."

Felicia looked at her but did not answer at once. Her lips were moving with a petition that came from a depth of feeling that measured a new life for her. She shook her head.

"No, I am going to stay. I shall take the pledge. I am ready to obey it. You do not understand why I am doing this, do you?"

Rose gave her one look, then turned and went out of the pew and down the aisle. She did not even stop to talk with her acquaintances. Mrs. Delano was going out of the church just as Rose stepped into the vestibule.

"So you are not going to join Dr. Bruce's volunteer company?" Mrs. Delano asked.

"No, I am not. It is simply absurd. I have always regarded the Raymond movement as fanatical."

"Yes, I understand it is resulting in a great deal of hardship in many cases. For my part, I believe Dr. Bruce has simply provoked disturbance here. It will result in splitting our church. You see if that isn't so. There are scores of people in the church who are so situated that they can't take such a pledge and keep it. I am one of them," she added as she went out with Rose.

When Rose reached home her father was standing in his usual attitude before the open fireplace, smoking a cigar. "Where is Felicia?" he asked as Rose came in alone.

"She stayed for an after-meeting," replied Rose shortly.

She threw off her wraps and was going upstairs when Mr. Sterling called after her, "An after-meeting? What do you mean?"

"Dr. Bruce asked the church to take the Raymond pledge."

Mr. Sterling took his cigar out of his mouth and twirled it nervously between his fingers.

"I didn't expect that of Dr. Bruce. Did many of the members stay?"

"I don't know," replied Rose. "I didn't." And she went upstairs, leaving her father standing in the drawing room.

After a few minutes he went to the window and stood there looking out at the people driving on the boulevard. His cigar had gone out, but he still fingered it nervously Then he turned from the window and walked up and down the room. When a servant stepped across the hall and announced dinner, he told her to wait for Felicia. Rose came downstairs and went into the library. And still Mr. Sterling paced the drawing room restlessly.

He had finally wearied of the walking and, throwing himself into a chair, was brooding deeply over something when Felicia came in.

He rose and faced her. Felicia had obviously been moved by the meeting from which she had just come. At the same time she was reluctant to talk about it.

"How many stayed?" he asked.

"About a hundred," replied Felicia gravely. Mr. Sterling looked surprised. Felicia was going out of the room but he called to her.

"Do you really mean to keep the pledge?" he asked.

Felicia felt her cheeks grow hot as she answered. "You would not ask such a question, Father, if you had been at the meeting." She then asked to be excused from dinner for a while and went to see her mother.

Felicia tried to describe to her mother something of the spiritual power that had awed every one of the company of disciples who faced Dr. Bruce in that meeting after the morning service. Felicia had never had such an experience before and never would have thought of sharing it with her mother, had it not been for the prayer the previous evening.

When she finally joined her father and Rose at the table, however, she felt reluctant to speak of it, as one might hesitate to describe a wonderful sunset to a person who never talked about anything but bad weather.

When that Sunday in the Sterling mansion was drawing to a close, Felicia knelt by her bed; and when she raised her face and turned it toward the light, it was the face of a woman who had already defined for herself the greatest issues of earthly life.

That same evening Dr. Bruce was talking over the events of the day with his wife. They were of one heart and mind in the matter, and faced their new future with all the faith and courage of new disciples. Neither was deceived as to the probable results of the pledge to themselves or to the church.

They had been talking but a little while when the doorbell ring. Dr. Bruce exclaimed as he opened it, "It's you, Edward! Come in!"

There entered the hall a commanding figure. Bishop Edward Hampton was of extraordinary height and breadth of shoulder, but of such good proportions that few were conscious of his unusual size. The impression the bishop made on strangers was first of good health, and then of great warmth.

He came into the parlor and greeted Mrs. Bruce, who soon departed discreetly, leaving the men alone.

The two men sat in deep easy chairs before the open fire. There was just enough dampness in the early spring of the year to make an open fire pleasant.

"Calvin, you have taken a very serious step today," the bishop said at last, turning his large dark eyes to his old college classmate's face. "I heard of it this afternoon. I could not resist the desire to see you about it tonight."

"I'm glad you came." Dr. Bruce felt a slight tremor in his stomach. "You understand what this means, Edward?

"I think I do. Yes, I'm sure I do." The bishop spoke slowly and thoughtfully. He sat with his hands clasped together.

Over his face, marked with lines of consecration and service and love of men, a shadow crept—a shadow not caused by the firelight. Again he gazed at his old friend.

"Calvin, we have always understood each other. Ever since our paths led us in different ways in church life, we have walked together in Christian fellowship."

"It is true," replied Dr. Bruce, with an emotion he made no attempt to conceal or subdue. "Thank God for it. I prize your fellowship more than any man's. I have always known what it meant, though it has always been more than I deserve."

The bishop looked affectionately at his friend. But the shadow still rested on his face. After a pause he spoke again.

"The new discipleship means a crisis for you in your work. If you keep this pledge to do all things as Jesus would do—as I know you will—it requires no prophet to predict some remarkable changes in your parish." The bishop looked wistfully at his friends and then continued.

"In fact, I do not see how a perfect upheaval of Christianity, as we now know it, can be prevented if the ministers and churches generally take the Raymond pledge and live it out." He paused as if he were waiting for his friend to say something, to ask some question. But Bruce did not know of the fire that was burning in the bishop's heart over the very question that he himself and Maxwell had fought out.

"Now in my church," continued the bishop, "it would be rather a difficult matter, I fear, to find very many people who would take a pledge like that and live up to it. Martyrdom is a lost art with us. Our Christianity loves its ease and comfort too well to take up anything so rough and heavy as a cross. And yet what does Jesus mean? What is it to walk in His steps?"

The bishop was soliloquizing now, and it is doubtful if he thought for the moment of his friend's presence. For the first time there flashed into Dr. Bruce's mind a suspicion of the truth. What if the bishop should throw the weight of his great influence on the side of the Raymond movement? He had the following of the most aristocratic and wealthy people, not only in Chicago, but in several large cities. What if the bishop should join this new discipleship?

The thought was about to be followed by the word. Dr. Bruce reached out his hand and, with the familiarity of life-long friendship, placed it on the bishop's shoulder ready to ask an important question, when they were both startled by the violent ringing of the bell. Mrs. Bruce went to the door and could be heard talking with someone in the hall. There was a loud exclamation and then, as the bishop rose and Dr. Bruce was stepping toward the curtain that hung before the entrance to the parlor, Mrs. Bruce pushed it aside. Her face was white and she was trembling.

"Oh, Calvin! Such terrible news! Mr. Sterling—oh, I cannot tell it! What a blow to those two girls!"

"What is it?" Dr. Bruce advanced with the bishop into the hall and confronted the messenger, a servant from the Sterlings. The man was without his hat, and had evidently run over with the news as Dr. Bruce lived nearest of any intimate friends of the family.

"Mr. Sterling shot himself, sir, a few minutes ago! He killed himself in his bedroom."

"I will go right over. Edward, will you go with me? The Sterlings are old friends of yours."

The bishop was very pale, but calm as always. He looked his friend in the face and answered, "Aye, Calvin, I will go with you, not only to this house of death, but also the whole way of human sin and sorrow, please God."

And even in that moment of horror at the unexpected news, Calvin Bruce understood what the bishop meant to do.

19

When Dr. Bruce and the bishop entered the Sterling mansion, everything in the usually well-appointed household was in the greatest confusion. The rooms downstairs were empty, but overhead were hurried footsteps and confused noises. One of the servants ran down the grand staircase with a look of horror on her face just as the bishop and Dr. Bruce were starting to go up.

"Miss Felicia is with Mrs. Sterling," the servant stammered in answer to a question, and then burst into tears and ran out of the room.

At the top of the staircase the two men were met by Felicia.

She walked up to Dr. Bruce at once and put both hands in his. The bishop laid his hands on her head and the three stood there a moment in perfect silence.

Bishop Hampton had known Felicia since she was a little child. He was the first to break silence.

"The God of all mercy be with you, Felicia, in this dark hour. Your mother—"

The bishop hesitated. Out of the buried past he had, during his hurried passage from his friends' house to this house of death, irresistibly drawn the one tender romance of his young manhood. Not even Bruce knew that. But there had been a time when the bishop had offered the incense of a singularly undivided affection to the beautiful Camilla Rolfe, and she had chosen between him and Sterling, the millionaire. The bishop carried no bitterness with this memory. But it was a memory still.

For the answer to the bishop's unfinished query, Felicia turned and went back into her mother's room. She had not said a word yet. But both men were struck with her wonderful calm. She returned to the hall door and beckoned to them, and the two ministers, with a feeling that they were about to behold something very unusual, entered.

Rose lay face down at the foot of the bed in a faint. Clara, the nurse, sat on the side of the bed with her head covered, sobbing. And Mrs. Sterling lay there so peaceful and still that at first the Bishop was deceived. Then, as the great truth broke upon him, the sharp agony of the old wound shot through his body. It passed and left him standing there in that chamber of death with the calmness and strength that all disciples of God have a need to possess.

The next moment the house below was in a tumult. Almost at the same time the doctor, who had been sent for at once but lived some distance away, came in together with police officers who had been summoned by the frightened servants. With them were four or five newspaper correspondents and several neighbors. Dr. Bruce and the bishop met

this miscellaneous crowd at the head of the stairs and succeeded in turning away all except those whose presence was
necessary.

Mr. Sterling had gone into his room that evening about
nine o'clock, and that was the last seen of him until, half-an-
hour later, a shot was heard in the room. A servant who was
in the hall ran into the room and found his master dead on
the floor, killed by his own hand. Felicia, at the time, was sitting by her mother. Rose was reading in the library. She ran
upstairs, saw her father as he was being lifted upon the couch
by the servants, and then ran screaming into her mother's
room, where she flung herself down on the foot of the bed
in a swoon. Mrs. Sterling had first fainted at the shock, then
rallied with wonderful swiftness and sent for Dr. Bruce. She
had then insisted on seeing her husband.

In spite of Felicia's protests, she had compelled Clara and
the housemaid, terrified and trembling, to support her while
she crossed the hall and entered the room where her husband
lay. She had looked upon him with a tearless face, returned
to her own room and laid down on her bed. Just as Dr. Bruce
and the bishop entered the house, Mrs. Sterling had died
with a prayer for forgiveness of herself and her husband on
her quivering lips. Felicia was bending over her and Rose
was still lying senseless at her feet.

Death had come swiftly and shockingly to the Sterling
palace of luxury that Sunday night. But the full cause of the
tragedy was not learned until the facts in regard to Mr. Sterling's business affairs were finally disclosed.

Then it was discovered that for some time he had been facing financial ruin, owing to certain speculations that had in a month's time swept away his supposed wealth. With the cunning and desperation of a man who battles for his very life, when he saw his money—all the life he ever valued—slipped from him, he had put off the evil day to the last moment.

Sunday afternoon, however, he had received news that proved to him beyond doubt the fact of his utter ruin. The very house that he called his, the chairs in which he sat, his carriage, the dishes from which he ate, had all been bought with money for which he himself had never really done an honest stroke of work.

It had all rested on a tissue of deceit and speculation that had no foundation in real values. He knew that fact better than anyone else, but had hoped, with the hope that such men always have, that the same methods that brought him the money would also prevent the loss. He had been deceived in this as many others have been. As soon as the truth that he was practically a beggar had dawned upon him, he saw no escape from suicide.

Mrs. Sterling's death was the result of shock. She had not been taken into her husband's confidence for years, but she knew that the sources of his wealth were precarious. Her health had been declining for several years. Mrs. Sterling illustrated the old family tradition when she was helped into the room where the body of her husband lay. But that feeble tenet could not sustain the spirit torn and weakened by long years of suffering and disappointment.

The effect of this triple blow—the death of father and mother and the loss of property—was instantly apparent in the sisters. The horror of events stupefied Rose for weeks. She did not yet seem to realize that the money that had been so large a part of her very existence was gone. Even when she was told that she and Felicia must leave the house and be dependent upon relatives and friends, she did not seem to understand what it meant.

Felicia, however, was fully conscious of the facts. She knew just what had happened and why. She was talking over her future plans with her cousin Rachel a few days after the funerals. Mrs. Winslow and Rachel had left Raymond and had come to Chicago as soon as the terrible news had reached them, and with other friends of the family they were planning for the future of Rose and Felicia.

"Felicia, you and Rose must come to Raymond with us. That is settled. Mother will not hear of any other plan at present," Rachel had said, her beautiful face glowing with love for her cousin.

"Unless I could find something to do here," answered Felicia.

She looked wistfully at Rachel and Rachel said gently, "What could you do, dear?"

"Nothing. I was never taught to do anything except a little music, and I do not know enough about it to teach it or earn my living at it. I have learned to cook a little," Felicia answered with a slight smile.

"Then you may cook for us. Mother is always having trouble with her kitchen," said Rachel, understanding well enough that Felicia needed some responsibility.

"May I? May I?" Felicia replied, as if it were to be considered seriously. "I am ready to do anything honorable to provide for my living and that of Rose."

"We will arrange the details when we get to Raymond," said Rachel.

So in a few weeks Rose and Felicia found themselves a part of the Winslow family in Raymond. It was a bitter experience for Rose, but there was nothing else for her to do, and she accepted the inevitable, brooding over the great change in her life and in many ways adding to the burden of Felicia and her cousin Rachel.

Felicia at once found herself in an atmosphere of discipleship that was like heaven to her in its revelation of companionship. Though Mrs. Winslow was not in sympathy with the course Rachel was taking, the remarkable events that had occurred since the pledge were too powerful in their results not to impress even such a woman as Mrs. Winslow.

With Rachel, Felicia found real fellowship. She soon was taking part in the new work at the Rectangle. In a short time she demonstrated her ability as a cook so clearly that Virginia suggested she take charge of the cooking class at the Rectangle.

Felicia entered upon this work with the keenest pleasure. For the first time in her life, she had the delight of doing something of value for others. Her resolve to act only after asking, "What would Jesus do?" touched her deepest nature.

Mrs. Winslow looked with astonishment upon her niece, this city-bred girl reared in the greatest luxury, now walking around in her kitchen, her arms covered with flour.

Occasionally there would be a streak of it on her nose (for Felicia at first had a habit of rubbing her nose when she was trying to remember some recipe). She mixed a variety of dishes with eager interest in their results, washed up pans and kettles and scrubbed floors both in the Winslow kitchen and the rooms of the Rectangle settlement.

At first Mrs. Winslow remonstrated, "Felicia, it is not your place to be out here doing this kind of work. I cannot allow it."

"Why, didn't you like the muffins I made this morning?" Felicia would ask meekly, but with a hidden smile, knowing her aunt's weakness for that kind of muffin.

"They were beautiful, Felicia. But it does not seem right for you to be doing such work for us."

"Why not? What else can I do?"

Her aunt looked at her thoughtfully, noting her remarkable beauty of face and expression.

"You do not always intend to do this sort of work, Felicia?"

"Maybe I shall. I have had a dream of opening a bakery shop in Chicago or some large city and going around to the poor families in the slum district like the Rectangle, teaching the mothers how to prepare food properly. I remember hearing Dr. Bruce say once that he believed one of the great miseries of poverty consisted in poor food. He even went so far as to say that he thought some kinds of crime could be traced to soggy biscuits and tough meat. I'm sure I would be able to make a living for Rose and myself, and at the same time help others."

Felicia pondered this dream constantly. Meanwhile, she grew into the affections of the Raymond people and the Rectangle folks, among whom she was known as the angel cook.

Three months had gone by since the Sunday morning when Dr. Bruce entered his pulpit with the message of the new discipleship. They were three months of excitement in Nazareth Avenue Church. There was the expected strong opposition from one segment of is congregation, yet the Reverend Bruce was deeply moved by an unexpected response from those men and women who, like Felicia, were hungry for something in their lives that conventional church membership and fellowship had failed to give them.

But Dr. Bruce was still restless and dissatisfied with himself when he met a second time with Bishop Hampton. The two friends seated themselves in Dr. Bruce's study.

"Do you know why I've come here this evening?" the bishop asked.

Dr. Bruce shook his head.

"I have come to confess that I have not yet kept my promise to walk in His steps in the way I believe I should."

Dr. Bruce had risen and was pacing his study. The bishop remained in the deep, easy chair, his hands clasped, his eyes burning with resolve.

"Edward"—Dr. Bruce spoke abruptly—"I have not yet been able to satisfy myself, either, in obeying my promise. But I have come face-to-face with the decision I feel I must make. In order to fulfill my pledge, I shall be obliged to resign from Nazareth Avenue Church."

"I knew you would," replied the bishop quietly. "And I

came this evening to say that I shall be obliged to do the same with my charge."

Dr. Bruce turned to his friend in surprise, both laboring under a repressed excitement.

"Is it necessary in your case?" asked Bruce.

"Yes. Let me state my reasons. Probably they are the same as yours. In fact, I am sure they are." The bishop paused a moment, then went on with increased feeling.

"Calvin, you known how many years I have been doing the work of my position, and you know something of the responsibility and the care of it. I do not mean to say that my life has been free from burden-bearing or sorrow. But I have certainly led what the poor and desperate of this sinful city would call a very comfortable—yes, a very luxurious life. I have had a beautiful house to live in, the most expensive food, clothing, and physical pleasures. I have been able to go abroad at least a dozen times, and have enjoyed for years the companionship of art and letters and music and all the very best. I have never known what it meant to be without money or its equivalent. And I have been unable to silence the question of late, 'What sacrifice have I made for the cause of Christ?'

"Paul was told what great things he must suffer for the sake of his Lord. Maxwell's position at Raymond is well-taken when he insists that to walk in the steps of Christ means to sacrifice something. Where has my suffering come in? The petty trials and annoyances of my clerical life are not worth mentioning as sorrows or suffering. Compared with Paul or any of the Christian martyrs or early disciples, I have lived a luxurious, sinful life, full of ease and pleasure. I cannot endure this any longer. I have not been walking in His steps. Under the present system of church and social life, I see no escape from this condemnation, except to give all I can of my life personally to the actual, physical, and soul needs of desperate people."

The bishop had risen now and walked over to the window. The street in front of the house was as light as day, and he looked out at the people passing, then turned, and with a passionate utterance that showed how deep the volcanic fire in him burned, he exclaimed, "Calvin, this is a terrible city in which we live. Its misery, its sin, its selfishness, appall my heart. And I have struggled for years with the sickening dread of the time when I should be forced to leave the pleasant luxury of my official position to put my life into contact with the modern paganism of this century.

"The awful working conditions of the girls in some factories, the brutal selfishness of an insolent society, fashion and wealth that ignores all the sorrows of the city, the fearful curse of liquor and gambling, the wail of the unemployed, the hatred of the church by countless men who see in it only great piles of costly stone and upholstered furniture and who look at the minister as a luxurious idler—all this in its contrast with the easy, comfortable life I have lived fills me more and more with a sense of mingled terror and self-accusation.

"I have heard the words of Jesus many times lately: 'Inasmuch as ye have done it unto the least of these, my brethren, ye have done it unto me.' And when have I personally visited the prisoner or desperate or sinful in any way that has actually caused me suffering? Rather, I have followed the conventional, soft habits of my position and have lived in the society of the rich, refined, aristocratic members of my congregations. What have I suffered for Jesus's sake?

"Do you know, Calvin"—he turned abruptly toward his friend—"I have been tempted of late to lash myself with a scourge. If I had lived in Martin Luther's time, I should have bared my back to a self-inflicted torture."

Dr. Bruce was very pale. Never had he seen his friend or heard him under the influence of such a passion. There was a sudden silence in the room. The bishop had sat down again and bowed his head. Dr. Bruce spoke at last.

"Edward, I do not need to say that you have expressed my feelings also. I have been in a similar position for years. My life has been one of comparative luxury. I do not, of course, mean to say that I have not had trials and discouragements and burdens in my church ministry. But I cannot say that I have sacrificed much for Jesus. That verse in Peter haunts me constantly: 'Christ also suffered for us, leaving us an example, that ye should follow his steps.'

"I have lived in luxury," continued Dr. Bruce. "I do not know what it means to want. I also have had my leisure for travel. I have been surrounded by the soft, easy comforts of civilization. The sin and misery of this great city has beat like waves against the stone walls of my church and of this house in which I live, and I have hardly heeded them, the walls have been so thick. I have reached a point where I cannot endure this any longer.

"I am not condemning the church. I love her. I am not forsaking the church. I believe in her mission and have no desire to destroy it. Least of all, in the step I am about to take, do I desire to be charged with abandoning the Christian fellowship.

"But I feel that I must resign my place as pastor of Nazareth Avenue Church in order to satisfy myself that I am walking as I ought to walk in His steps. In this action I judge no other ministers and pass no criticism on the discipleship of others. But I feel as you do. I must come personally into a closer contact with the sin and shame and degradation of this great city. And I know that to do this I must sever my immediate connection with Nazareth Avenue Church."

Again that sudden silence fell over these two men. It was no ordinary action they were deciding. They had both reached the same conclusion by the same reasoning, and they were too thoughtful and too accustomed to the measuring of conduct to underestimate the seriousness of their position.

"What is your plan?" The bishop spoke gently, looking up with a smile that always softened his face.

"My plan," replied Dr. Bruce slowly, "is, in brief, to put myself into the center of the greatest human need I can find in this city and live there. My wife is fully in accord with me. We have already decided to find a residence in that part of the city where we can make our personal lives count for the most."

"Let me suggest a place." Bishop Hampton was on fire now. Then he unfolded a plan of such far-reaching power and possibility that Dr. Bruce, capable and experienced as he was, felt amazed at the vision of a greater soul than his own.

They sat up late and were as eager, even glad, as if they were planning a trip to some exotic land of unexplored travel. Indeed, the bishop said many times afterward that the moment his decision was reached to live the life of personal sacrifice, he suddenly felt an uplifting as if a great burden had been taken from him. He was exultant. So was Dr. Bruce from the same cause.

20

Their plan as it finally grew into a workable fact was in reality nothing more than the renting of a large building formerly used as a warehouse for a brewery, reconstructing it and living in it themselves in the very heart of a territory where the saloon ruled with power, where the tenement was its filthiest, and where vice and ignorance and shame and poverty were congested into vicious forms.

It was not a new idea. It was an idea started by Jesus Christ when He left His Father's house in order to get nearer humanity, and by becoming part of its sin help to draw humanity apart from its sin. The university settlement idea is not modern. It is as old as Bethlehem and Nazareth. And in this particular case it was the nearest approach to anything that would satisfy the hunger of these two men to sacrifice for Christ.

There had sprung up in them at the same time a longing that amounted to a passion to get nearer the great physical poverty and spiritual destitution of the mighty city that throbbed around them. How could they do this except as they became a part of it, as nearly as one man can become a part of another's misery? Where was the suffering to come in unless there was an actual self-denial of some sort? And what was to make that self-denial apparent to themselves or anyone else unless it took this concrete, actual, personal form of trying to share the deepest suffering and sin of the city?

So they reasoned for themselves, not judging others. They were simply keeping their own pledge to do as Jesus would do, as they honestly judged He would do.

Everyone in Chicago knew that Bishop Hampton had a handsome fortune. Dr. Bruce had acquired and saved a substantial sum from literary work carried on in connection with his parish duties. The two friends agreed to put a large part of this money into the work, most of it into the furnishing of a Settlement House.

Meanwhile Nazareth Avenue Church was experiencing something never known before in all its history. The simple appeal on the part of its pastor to his members to do as Jesus would do had created a sensation that still continued. The result of that appeal was very much the same as in Henry Maxwell's church in Raymond, only this church was far more aristocratic, wealthy and conventional.

Nevertheless, when one Sunday morning in early summer Dr. Bruce came into the pulpit and announced his resignation, the sensation deepened all over the city. Dr. Bruce had consulted with his board of trustees so that the step he intended was not a matter of surprise to them.

But when it became publicly known that the bishop had also announced his resignation and retirement from the position he had held so long, in order to go and live in the center of the worst part of Chicago, public astonishment reached its height.

"But why?" the bishop replied to one valued friend, who had, almost with tears, tried to dissuade him from his purpose. "Why should what Dr. Bruce and I propose to do seem so remarkable a thing, as if it were unheard of that a doctor of divinity and a bishop should want to save souls in this particular manner? If we were to resign our charges for the purpose of going to Bombay or Hong Kong or any place in Africa, Christian people would applaud our missionary goals. Why should it seem any different for us to give our lives to help rescue the heathen and the lost of our own city? Is it, then, such a tremendous event that two Christian ministers should be not only willing but eager to live close to the misery of the world in order to know it and try to alleviate it?"

Though the bishop may have satisfied himself that there ought to be nothing so remarkable about it all, the public continued to talk and the churches to record their astonishment that two such men, so prominent in the ministry, should leave their comfortable homes, voluntarily resign their pleasant social positions and enter upon a life of hardship, self-denial, and actual suffering.

Nazareth Avenue Church parted from its pastor with regret, for the most part, although the regret was modified with a feeling of relief on the part of those who had refused to take the pledge

Dr. Bruce carried with him the respect of the men who, entangled in business in such a way that obedience to the pledge would have ruined them, still held in their deeper, better natures a genuine admiration for courage and consistency. They had known Dr. Bruce many years as a kindly, conservative, safe man; but the thought of him in the light of sacrifice of this sort was unfamiliar. As fast as they understood it, they gave their pastor the credit of being absolutely true to his recent convictions as to what following Jesus meant. Nazareth Avenue Church became a stronger church because of the movement started by Dr. Bruce.

It was fall again, and the city faced another hard winter. One afternoon the bishop came out of the Settlement and walked around the block, intending to visit one of his new friends in the district. He had walked about four blocks when he was attracted by a shop that looked different from the others. The neighborhood was still new to him, and every day he discovered some strange spot or stumbled upon some unexpected humanity.

The place that attracted his notice was a small house close by a Chinese laundry. There were two windows in the front, very clean, which was remarkable to begin with. Inside the window was a tempting display of cookery with prices attached to the various foods. This made him wonder, since he was familiar by now with many facts in the lives of the people who were once unknown to him.

As he stood looking at the windows, the door between them opened and Felicia Sterling came out.

"Felicia!" exclaimed the bishop. "When did you move into my parish without my knowledge?"

"How did you find me so soon?" asked Felicia.

"Why, don't you know? These are the only clean windows in the block."

"I believe they are," replied Felicia with a laugh that did the bishop good to hear.

"But why have you dared come to Chicago without telling me, and how have you entered my diocese without my knowledge?" asked the bishop. Felicia looked so like that beautiful, clean, educated, refined world he once knew that he might be pardoned for seeing in her something of the old paradise.

"Well, dear Bishop," said Felicia, "I knew how overwhelmed you were with your work. I did not want to burden you with my plans. And besides, I was just on my way to see you, offer my services and ask your advice. I am settled here for the present with Mrs. Bascom, a saleswoman who rents us three rooms, and with one of Rachel's music pupils, who is being helped to a course in violin by Virginia Page.

"She is from the people," continued Felicia, using the words *from the people* so gravely and unconsciously that her hearer smiled. "And I am keeping house for her, and at the same time beginning an experiment in good food for the poor. I am an expert and have a plan I want you to admire and develop. Will you, dear Bishop?"

"Indeed I will," he replied. The sight of Felicia and her vitality, enthusiasm, and purpose almost bewildered him.

"Martha can help at the Settlement with her violin and I will help with my recipes. You see, I thought I would get settled first and then come to you with something specific to offer. I'm able to earn my own living now."

"You are?" Bishop Hampton asked a little incredulously. "How? Making those things?"

" 'Those things'!" exclaimed Felicia with a show of indignation. "I would have you know, sir that 'those things' are the best-cooked, purest food products in this whole city."

"I don't doubt it," he replied hastily, while his eyes twinkled.

"Come in and try some," she exclaimed. "You poor bishop! You look as if you hadn't had a good meal for a month."

She insisted on his entering the little front room where Martha, a wide-awake girl with short, curly hair, was busy with her music practice.

"Go right on, Martha. This is the bishop. You have heard me speak of him often. Sit down there, Bishop, and let me give you a taste of something special, for I believe you have been actually fasting."

So they had an improvised lunch, and the bishop, who to tell the truth had not taken time for weeks to enjoy his meals, was delighted at the quality of the cooking. "Felicia, do you mean that you will live here and help these people to know the value of good food?"

"Indeed I do," she answered gravely. "That is my gospel. Shall I not follow it?"

"You're right. Bless God for sense like yours. When I left the world"—the bishop smiled at the phrase—"they were talking a good deal about the 'new woman.' If you are one of them, I am a convert right here and now."

Felicia laughed gaily. And the bishop's heart, heavy though it had grown during several months of vast burden-bearing, rejoiced to hear it. The laughter sounded good. It was good. It belonged to God.

Felicia wanted to visit the Settlement and went back with him. She was amazed at what money and a good deal of consecrated brains had done. As they walked through the building they talked incessantly. She was the incarnation of vital enthusiasm, and he marveled at it as it bubbled up and overflowed.

They went down into the basement and the bishop pushed open a door, behind which there came the sound of a carpenter's plane. It was a small but well-equipped workshop. A young man clad in shirt and overalls was driving the plane as he whistled. He looked up as the two entered.

"Miss Sterling, Mr. Stephen Clyde," said the bishop. "Clyde is one of our helpers here two afternoons a week."

Just then the bishop was called upstairs and he excused himself for a moment, leaving Felicia and the young carpenter together.

'I'm surprised to see you here," said Felicia, a faint color appearing on her cheeks. "And glad, too."

"Are you?" The flush of pleasure mounted to the young carpenter's forehead. "You have had a great deal of trouble lately," he said, and then regretted that he had called up a painful memory.

"Yes, but that is in the past. How is that you are working here?"

"It is a long story, Felicia. My father lost his money and I was obliged to go to work. A very good thing for me. The bishop says I ought to be grateful. And I am. I'm learning this trade, hoping sometime to be of use. I am also a night clerk at the Windsor Hotel. That Sunday morning when you took the pledge at Nazareth Church, I took it with the others."

"Did you?" said Felicia slowly. "I'm glad."

Just then the bishop came back, and soon he and Felicia left, leaving the young carpenter at his work, whistling louder than ever.

"Felicia," said the bishop, "did you know Stephen Clyde before?"

"Yes," replied Felicia. "He was one of my acquaintances at Nazareth Avenue Church."

"Ah!"

"We were good friends," added Felicia.

"But nothing more?"

Felicia's eyes sparkled for an instant. Then she looked her companion in the eyes frankly and answered, "Just friends."

It would be just the thing for those two young people to come to like each other, thought the bishop to himself, and somehow the thought made him grave. It was almost like the old pang he felt over Camilla. But it passed, leaving him a bit sad. *After all*, he reasoned, *is not romance a part of humanity? Love is older than I am, and wiser*.

The following week the bishop had an experience that belongs to this part of the Settlement's history.

He was coming back to the Settlement very late from a meeting, and was walking along with his hands behind him when two men jumped out from behind an old fence that shut off an abandoned factory from the street and faced him. One of the men thrust a pistol into his face.

"Hold up your hands and be quick about it!" he said.

The place was lonely and the bishop entertained no thought of resistance. He did as he was commanded, and the other man began to go through his pockets. He was calm. His nerves did not quiver. As he stood there with his arms uplifted, an unknowing spectator might have thought that he was praying for the souls of these two men. In fact, the bishop was.

Since the bishop was not in the habit of carrying much money with him, the man searching him uttered an oath at the small amount of change he found. Then the man with the pistol growled, "Grab his watch! We might as well get all we can out of the job!"

Suddenly there came the sound of footsteps.

"Get behind the fence!" hissed the man with the pistol, making a menacing gesture with it. With his companion, he pushed the bishop down the alley and through a ragged, broken opening in the fence. The three stood still there in the shadows until the footsteps passed.

"Now then, have you got the watch?" asked the man with the pistol.

"No, the chain is caught somewhere." And the other man swore again.

"Break it, then!"

"No, don't break it," said the bishop, and it was the first time he had spoken. "The chain is the gift of a very dear friend. I should be sorry to have it broken."

At the sound of the bishop's voice, the man with the pistol started. With a quick movement of his free hand he turned the bishop's head toward what little light was shining from the alleyway, at the same time taking a step nearer. Then he said roughly, "Leave the watch alone. We've got the money. That's enough!"

"Enough? There's only fifty cents!"

"Leave that watch be. And put back the money, too. This is the bishop we've held up. The bishop, do you hear?"

"What of it? I don't care if he's the President of the United States."

"I say put the money back, or in five seconds I'll blow a hole through your head that'll let in more sense than you have now."

For a second the robber seemed to hesitate at this strange turn in events, as if measuring his companion's intention. Then he dropped the money back into the rifled pocket.

"You can take your hands down, sir." The man lowered his weapon, still keeping an eye on the other man and speaking with rough respect. The bishop brought his arms to his side slowly and looked earnestly at the two men. In the dim light it was difficult to distinguish features. He was evidently free to go his way now, but he continued to stand, making no movement.

"You can go on. You needn't stay any longer on our account." The man who had acted as spokesman was suddenly nervous and uncertain. The other man stood by angrily.

"That's just what I am staying for," replied the bishop.

There was an uneasy silence.

"If you would only allow me to be of help . . ." said Bishop Hampton gently, even lovingly. The man with the pistol stared at him through the darkness. After a moment of silence, he spoke slowly, like one who had finally decided upon a course he had at first rejected.

"Do you remember ever seeing me before?"

"No," said the bishop. "The light isn't very good and I haven't really had a good look at you."

"Do you know me now?" The man suddenly took off his hat and walked over to the bishop until they were near enough to touch each other. The man's hair was coal black except for one white spot on the top of his head about as large as the palm of the hand.

The minute the bishop saw that spot he started. A past memory began to stir in him. The man helped him.

"Don't you remember one day fifteen years ago when a man came to your house and told about his wife and child having been burned to death in a tenement fire in New York?"

"Yes, I begin to remember."

"Do you remember how you took me into your own house that night and spent all next day trying to find me a job? And how, when you succeeded in getting me a place in a warehouse as foreman, I promised to quit drinking because you asked me to?"

"I do remember it. I hope you have kept your promise?"

The man laughed hoarsely. Then he struck his hand against the fence with such sudden passion that he drew blood.

"Keep it! I was drunk inside a week. I've been drinking ever since. But I've never forgotten you or your prayer. Do you remember the morning after I came to your house and you sat down with me after breakfast and prayed with me?

That got me! My mother used to pray. I can see her now, kneeling down by my bed when I was a lad. Father came in one night and kicked her while she was kneeling there by me. But I never forgot that prayer of yours that morning.

"You prayed for me just as Mother used to," he continued, "and you didn't seem to be bothered by the fact that I was more than half-drunk when I rang your doorbell. Since then, the saloon has housed me and made hell on earth for me. But that prayer stuck to me all the time. My promise not to drink was broken into a thousand pieces inside of two Sundays, and I lost the job you found for me, and landed in the police station two days afterward; but I never forgot you or your prayer. I don't know what good it has done me, but I never forgot it. And I won't do any harm to you, nor let anyone else. So you're free to go. That's why."

The bishop did not stir. Somewhere a church clock struck one. He was thinking hard.

"How long is it since you had work?" he asked.

"More than six months since either of us did anything to speak of. Unless you call robbing people work."

"Suppose I found jobs for both of you. Would you quit this and begin all over?"

"What's the use?" The other man spoke sullenly. "I've reformed a hundred times. Every time I go down deeper. It's too late."

"No!" said the bishop. And never before had he felt the desire to salvage people burn in him so strongly. All the time he sat there during the remarkable scene, he prayed, "O Lord

Jesus, give me the souls of these two for Thee. I am hungry for them. Give them to me."

"No," the bishop repeated. "What does God want of you two men? It doesn't so much matter what I want. You two men are of infinite value to Him." And then his wonderful memory came to his aid and he remembered the man's name.

"Burns," he said, "if you and your friend here will go home with me tonight, I will find you both places of honorable employment. I will believe in you and trust you. You are both young men. Why should God lose you? It is a great thing to win the love of the great Father.

"It is a small thing that I should love you. But if you need to feel again that there is love in the world, you will believe me when I say, my brothers, that I love you, and in the name of Him who was crucified for our sins I cannot bear to see you miss the glory of the human life. Come. Be men. Make another try for it, God helping you. No one but God and you and myself need ever know anything of this tonight. He has forgiven it. The minute you ask Him to, you will find that true. Come! We'll fight it out together, you and I."

And the bishop broke into a prayer to God that was a continuation of his appeal to the men. His pent-up feeling could find no other outlet.

Before he had prayed many moments Burns was sitting with his face buried in his hands, sobbing. And the other man, harder, less moved, without a previous knowledge of the bishop, leaned back against the fence, stolid at first. But as the prayer went on, the Holy Spirit swept over his dulled, brutal, coarsened life. This same supernatural Presence that smote Paul on the road to Damascus and poured through Henry Maxwell's church and then broke irresistibly over the Nazareth Avenue congregation now manifested Himself in this dark corner of a mighty city over two sinful, sunken men. The prayer seemed to break open the crust that had for years kept them from divine communication. And they themselves were thoroughly startled by it.

The bishop finished praying, and at first did not realize himself what had happened. Neither did they. Burns still sat with his head bowed between his knees. The other man leaning against the fence looked at the bishop with awe.

The bishop took charge.

"Come, by brothers. God is good. You shall stay at the Settlement tonight. And I will make good my promise as to the work."

The two men followed him in silence. When they reached the Settlement, it was after two in the morning. He let them in and led them to a room, pausing only a moment before leaving. His tall, commanding figure filled the doorway, and his pale face, though worn with his recent experiences, was illuminated with love and joy.

"God bless you, my brothers," he said, leaving them his benediction.

In the morning he almost dreaded to face the men. But the impression of the night had not worn away. True to his promise, he secured work for them. The janitor of the Settlement needed an assistant, owing to the growth of the work there. So Burns was given that place. The bishop succeeded in getting his companion a position as driver for a shipping firm not far from the Settlement. And the Holy Spirit, struggling in these two men, began a work of regeneration.

That very afternoon Burns was installed in his new position as assistant janitor. While he was cleaning off the front steps of the Settlement, he paused a moment and stood to look about him.

The first thing he noticed was a beer sign just up the street, next to the Settlement. He could almost touch it with his broom. Across the street were two large saloons, and a little farther down three more.

Suddenly the door of the nearby saloon opened and a man came out. At the same time two more went in. The enticing odor of beer floated up to Burns as he stood on the steps.

He clutched his broom handle tightly and began to sweep again, one foot on the porch and another on the step just below. He took another step down, still sweeping. By now the sweat stood on his forehead, although the day was frosty and the air chill. The saloon door opened again and three or four men came out. Then a child went in with a pail and came out a moment later with a quart of beer. As the child went by him on the sidewalk, the odor of beer was overwhelming. He took another step down, still sweeping desperately. His fingers were purple as he clutched the handle of the broom.

Suddenly he pulled himself up by a tremendous effort to the porch and went over to the corner farthest from the saloon and began to sweep there. "O God!" he cried. "If only the bishop would come back!" The bishop had gone out with Dr. Bruce somewhere, and there was no one about that Burns knew.

He swept in the corner for two or three minutes, his face drawn with the agony of the conflict. Gradually he edged out again toward the steps and began to descend. He looked toward the sidewalk and saw that he had left one step unswept. The sight seemed to give him a reasonable excuse for going down there to finish his sweeping. He was on the sidewalk now, sweeping the last step, with his face toward the Settlement and his back turned partly on the saloon nearby. He swept the step a dozen times. The sweat rolled over his face. He could smell the beer and rum, as the fumes rose around him.

He was down in the middle of the sidewalk now, still sweeping. He cleared the space in front of the Settlement and even went out into the gutter and swept that. He took off his hat and rubbed his sleeve over his face. His lips were pallid and his teeth chattered. His soul shook within him.

He crossed over the little piece of stone flagging that separated the saloon from the Settlement, and now stood in front of the saloon, looking at the sign and staring into the window at the pile of bottles arranged in a great pyramid inside. Moistening his lips with his tongue, he took a step forward, looking around him stealthily. The door suddenly opened again and someone came out. Again the hot, penetrating smell of liquor swept out into the cold air, and he took another step toward the saloon door, which had shut behind the customer. As he laid his fingers on the door handle, a tall figure came around the corner. It was Bishop Hampton.

Burns felt a strong hand on his arm. He tried to shake it off, now in a frenzy for drink. When the bishop held on tightly, Burns struck at his friend savagely. The blow fell upon the bishop's face and his signet ring cut a gash in his cheek.

The bishop never said a word, though over his face there spread a look of majestic sorrow. He picked Burns up as if he had been a child and actually carried him up the steps and into the Settlement House. Putting him down in the hall, the bishop shut the door and put his back against it.

Burns fell on his knees, sobbing. The bishop stood there panting with exertion, although Burns was a slightly built man and not a great weight for a man of his strength to carry. He was moved with unspeakable pity.

"Pray, Burns. Pray as you never prayed before. Nothing else will save you."

"O God, save me!" cried Burns. "Oh, save me from my hell!" And the bishop knelt by him in the hall and prayed with him.

After that they rose, and Burns went to his room. He came out of it that evening like a humble child. And the bishop went his way, older from that experience, with a wound on his face that would be a lifetime scar. Truly he was learning something of what it meant to walk in His steps.

21

Bishop Hampton and Dr. Bruce were troubled about the close proximity of the saloon to the Settlement. It would be a constant source of temptation to Burns.

"Did you eve make any inquiries about the ownership of this property adjoining us?" the bishop asked.

"No, I haven't taken time for it. I will now, if you think it would be worthwhile. But what can we do, Edward, against the liquor interests? They are as firmly established as the churches or politics."

"God will handle it in time, just as He removed slavery," replied the bishop gravely. "Meanwhile, I think we have a right to know who controls this saloon so near the Settlement."

"I'll find out," said Dr. Bruce.

Two days later he walked into the business office of one of the members of Nazareth Avenue Church and asked to see him for a few moments. He was received by his old parishioner, Clayton Price, who welcomed him warmly.

"I called to see you about that property next to the Settlement where the bishop and I now work. I am going to speak plainly, because life is too short and too serious for us both to have any foolish hesitation about this matter. Clayton, do you think it is right to rent that property for a saloon?"

Dr. Bruce's question was as direct and uncompromising as he had meant it to be. The effect of it on his old parishioner was instantaneous.

First a hot flush rose to the face of the businessman. Then he grew pale and dropped his head on his hands. When he raised it again, Dr. Bruce was amazed to see a tear roll down his cheek.

"Doctor, did you know that I took the pledge that morning with the others?"

"Yes, I remember."

"But you never knew how I have been tormented over my failure to keep it. That saloon property has been the temptation of the devil to me. It is the best-paying investment I have at present. And yet it was only a minute before you came in here that I was in an agony of remorse to think how I was letting this earthly gain tempt me into a denial of the very Christ I promised to follow. I know well enough that He would never rent property for such a purpose. There is no need, Doctor, for you to say a word more."

Dr. Bruce stood up, embraced his former parishioner and departed.

Within a month the saloon next to the Settlement closed. The saloon-keeper's lease had expired, and Clayton Price not only refused to renew it, but offered the building to the bishop and Dr. Bruce to use for their work, which had now grown so large that the building they had first rented was insufficient for all the projects that were planned.

One of the most important of these was the special food department suggested by Felicia. It was not a month after Clayton turned the saloon property over to the Settlement that Felicia found herself installed—in what had formerly been the main barroom—as head of a department of cooking and a course in housekeeping for girls who wished to make a living as servants. She was now a resident of the Settlement along with the Bruces and the bishop, Burns and his friend, and other women from the city. Martha, the violinist, came over to the Settlement on certain evenings to give lessons in music.

"Felicia, tell us your plan in full now," said the bishop one evening when he, Dr. and Mrs. Bruce and Felicia were together.

"Well, I have long thought of the hired-girl problem," said Felicia. "And I have reached certain conclusions in regard to it which you men may not grasp, though I'm sure Mrs. Bruce will understand me."

"We acknowledge our inadequacy, Felicia. Go on," said the bishop with a smile.

"Then this is what I propose to do. The old saloon building is large enough to divide into a suite of rooms that would be the equivalent of an ordinary house. My plan is to teach housekeeping and cooking to girls who will afterwards go out into service. The course will be ten weeks long. In that time I will teach plain cooking, neatness, quickness, and a love of good work."

"Hold on, Felicia!" the bishop interrupted. "This is not an age of miracles!"

"Then we will make it one," replied Felicia. "I know this seems like an impossibility, but I want to try it. I know a score of girls already who will take the course. And if we can once establish something like an *esprit de corps* among the girls themselves, I am sure it will be of great value to them."

"Felicia, if you can accomplish half of what you propose, it will bless this community," said Mrs. Bruce. "I don't see how you can do it, but I say God bless you as you try."

Felicia's plan succeeded beyond all expectations. In time the graduates of Felicia's cooking school came to be prized by housekeepers all over the city. But that is anticipating our story! The history of the Settlement has never yet been written. When it is, Felicia's part will be found of very great importance.

The depth of winter found Chicago presenting, as every great city of the world presents to the eyes of Christendom, the marked contrast between riches and poverty; between culture, refinement, luxury and ease, and ignorance, depravity, destitution, and the bitter struggle for bread.

It was a hard winter but a gay one. Never had here been such a succession of parties, receptions, balls, dinners, banquets. Never had the opera and theatre been so crowded with fashionable audiences. Never had there been such a lavish display of jewels and dresses.

And never, on the other hand, had the deep want and suffering been so cruel. Never had the wind blown so chillingly over the lake and through the thin shells of tenements in the neighborhood of the Settlement. Never had the pressure for food and fuel and clothes been so urgently thrust up against the people of the city.

Bishop Hampton and Dr. Bruce, with their assistants, went out and helped save men, women, and children from the torture of physical privation. Substantial quantities of food and clothing and money were donated by the churches, charitable societies, civic authorities, and benevolent associations. But the personal touch of the Christian disciple was hard to secure. Where were the disciples obeying the Master's command to go to the suffering and give themselves with their gifts in order to make these gifts of value in time to come?

The bishop found his heart sinking within him as he faced this fact: that men would give money who would not think of giving themselves. And the money they gave did not represent any real sacrifice because they did not miss it. They gave what was easiest to give, what hurt them the least. Where did the sacrifice come in? Was this following Jesus? Was this going with Him all the way?

The bishop was appalled to discover how few of his wealthy friends would really suffer any genuine inconvenience for the sake of humanity. Is charity the giving of worn-out garments? Is the gift really a gift when simply turned over to a paid solicitor or secretary of some benevolent organization? Shall the man never go and give his gift himself? Shall the woman never deny herself her reception or party or musicale and go personally and actually touch humanity as it festers in the great metropolis?

All this the bishop asked himself as he plunged deeper into the sin and sorrow of that bitter winter. He was bearing his cross with joy. And still, silently, powerfully, irresistibly, the Holy Spirit was moving through the churches, touching aristocratic, wealthy, ease-loving members who shunned the terrors of the social problems as they would shun a contagious disease.

This fact was impressed upon the Settlement workers in a startling way one morning. Perhaps no other incident that winter could have shown more plainly how much momentum had already grown out of the movement of Nazareth Avenue Church and the action of Dr. Bruce and Bishop Hampton following the pledge to do as Jesus would do.

The breakfast hour at the Settlement was the one hour in the day when the whole family found a little breathing space for fellowship together. It was an hour of relaxation. There was a great deal of good-natured repartee and much real wit and enjoyable fun at this hour. The bishop told his best stories. Dr. Bruce was at his best in description. This company of disciples was healthily humorous, in spite of the atmosphere of sorrow that constantly surrounded them. In fact, the bishop often said that the faculty of humor was as God-given as any other, and in his own case it was the only safety valve he had for the tremendous pressures put upon him.

This particular morning he was reading extracts from a morning paper for the benefit of the others. Suddenly he paused, and his face grew gray and sad. The rest looked up and a hush fell over the table.

"Man is shot and killed while taking a lump of coal from a coal car," he read. "His family was freezing and he had had no work for six months. His six children and a wife all packed into a three-room cabin on the West Side. One child wrapped in rags in a closet!"

These were the headlines that the Bishop read aloud. He went on to read the detailed account of the shooting and the visit of the reporter to the tenement where the family lived.

When he finished, there was silence around the table. The humor of the hour was swept away by this bit of human tragedy.

There were various comments on the part of the residents. One of the newcomers, a young man preparing for the ministry, said, "Why didn't the man apply to one of the charity organizations for help? Or to the city? It is certainly not true that, even at its worst, this city full of Christian people would knowingly allow anyone to go without food or fuel."

"No, I don't believe it would," replied Dr. Bruce. "But we don't know the history of this man's case. He may have asked for help so often before that finally, in a moment of desperation, he determined to help himself. I have known such cases this winter."

"That is not the most terrible fact in this case," said the bishop. "The worst thing about it is the fact that the man had not had any work for six months."

"Why don't such people go out into the country?" asked the divinity student.

Someone at the table, who had made a special study of the opportunities for work in the country, answered the question. According to him, the places in the country that might provide steady employment were exceedingly few, and in almost every case offered only to men without families. Suppose a man's wife and children were ill. How could he move or get into the country? How could he pay even the meager sum necessary to move his few goods? There were probably a hundred reasons why this particular man had not gone elsewhere.

"Meanwhile, there are the wife and children," said Mrs. Bruce. "How awful! Where is the place, did they say?"

"Why, it's only three blocks from here. This is the Penrose district. I believe Penrose himself owns half of the houses in that block. They are among the worst houses in this part of the city. And Penrose is a church member."

"Yes, he belongs to the Nazareth Avenue Church," replied Dr. Bruce in a low voice.

The bishop rose from the table, the very figure of divine wrath. He had just opened his mouth to say something when the bell rang and one of the residents went to the door.

"Tell Dr. Bruce I want to see him," came a voice. "Penrose is the name. Clarence Penrose. Dr. Bruce knows me."

22

Clarence Penrose was from an aristocratic family of great wealth and social distinction. He had large property holdings in different parts of the city. For many years he had been a member of Dr. Bruce's church.

Now both Dr. Bruce and Bishop Hampton left the table and went into the hall to greet him.

"Come in, Clarence," said Dr. Bruce, and they ushered the visitor into the reception room and closed the door.

Penrose faced the two ministers with a look of agitation on his pale face. His lip trembled as he spoke. It was an unusual occasion that would put Clarence Penrose in the position of showing any emotion or agitation.

"Did you read about the shooting? The family lived in one of my houses. It's a terrible thing. But that is not the primary reason for my visit." He looked nervously into the faces of the two men.

"Dr. Bruce!" he exclaimed, with almost a child's terror in his voice. "I came to say that I have had an experience so unusual that nothing but the supernatural can explain it. You remember I was one of those who took the pledge to do as Jesus would do. I thought at the time, poor fool that I was, that I had been doing the Christian thing all along. I gave liberally out of my abundance to the church and charity. I never gave myself, though.

"So I have been living in a perfect hell of contradictions ever since I took the pledge. My little girl—Diana, you remember—also took the pledge. She has been asking me a great many questions lately about the poor people and where they live. I have been obliged to answer her. Her questions last night touched me sorely: 'Do you own any houses where those people live? Are they nice and warm like ours?' You know how a child will ask questions like that.

"Well, I went to bed tormented with what I now know to be the divine arrows of conscience. I could not sleep. I seemed to see the Judgment Day. I was placed before the Judge. I was asked to give an account of the good deeds I had performed personally. What had I done with my stewardship? How about those tenements where people froze in winter and stifled in summer? Did I give any thought to them, except to receive the rentals from them? Would Jesus have done as I had done and was doing? How had I used the money and culture and social influence I possessed? Had I used it to bless humanity, to relieve the suffering, to bring joy to the distressed and hope to the despondent? I had received much. How much had I given?

"All this came to me in a waking vision as distinctly as I see you two men now. I was unable to see the end of the vision. I had a confused picture in my mind of the suffering

Christ pointing a condemning finger at me, and the rest was shut out by mist and darkness. I have not slept for 24 hours. The first thing I saw this morning was the account of the shooting at the coal yards. I read the account with a feeling of horror I have not been able to shake off. I am a guilty creature before God."

Penrose paused suddenly. The two men looked at him solemnly. What power of the Holy Spirit had moved the soul of this hitherto self-satisfied, elegant, cultured man? The bishop laid his hand on the shoulder of the distraught Penrose and said, "My brother, God has been very near to you. Let us thank Him."

"Yes, yes," sobbed Penrose. He sat down on a chair and covered his face. The bishop prayed. Then Penrose quietly rose and asked, "Will you go with me to that house?"

In reply, the two men put on their overcoats and went out with him to the home of the dead man's family.

This was the beginning of a new and strange life for Clarence Penrose. From the moment he stepped into that wretched hovel of a home and faced—for the first time in his life—suffering such as he had only read about, he was launched into a new life.

It began with his finding a home for the fatherless family of seven and providing for their care. Then he began a systematic personal inspection of all his properties to see that they were properly maintained, with adequate heat. That was just the beginning of a series of adventures during the following months that resulted from his questioning, "What would Jesus do?"

Before that winter reached its bitter climax, other events occurred in the city that concerned the lives of all the people who had promised to walk in His steps.

One afternoon Felicia came out of the Settlement with a basket of food samples for a baker in the Penrose district, just as Stephen Clyde emerged from the carpenter shop.

"Let me carry your basket, please," he said.

"Why do you say please?" asked Felicia, handing over the basket as they walked along.

"I would like to say something else," said Stephen, glancing at her with a boldness that frightened him. For he had been thinking of Felicia constantly, ever since he first saw her that day with the bishop. And for weeks now he had found many ways to be in her company.

"What else?" asked Felicia innocently.

"Why," said Stephen, turning full toward her and eyeing her with admiration, "I would like to say, 'Let me carry your basket, Felicia, dear.'"

Felicia walked on a little way without even turning her face toward him. Finally she turned and said shyly, "Why don't you say it, then?"

"May I?" cried Stephen, and the container tipped so precariously that Felicia exclaimed, "Yes, but watch the basket!"

"Why, I wouldn't think of dropping anything so important," said Stephen, promptly swinging the basket so high that Felicia squealed in protest.

Hours later the bishop was walking along a rather secluded spot near the outlying part of the Settlement district when he heard a familiar voice: "But tell me, Felicia, when did you begin to love me?"

"I fell in love with a little pine shaving just above your ear that day when I saw you in the shop!" said the other voice with a tinkly laugh.

The next moment the bishop turned the corner and came upon them.

"Where are you going with that basket?" he asked in amusement.

"We're taking it to—Where are we taking it to, Felicia?"

"Dear bishop, I guess now we're taking it home to begin—"

"To begin housekeeping," finished Stephen.

"Are you, now?" said the bishop. "I hope you will invite me in to share it. I know how good Felicia's cooking is."

"Bishop, dear Bishop," said Felicia, and she did not pretend to hide her happiness, "indeed, you shall always be the most honored guest. Are you glad?"

"I certainly am," he replied, interpreting Felicia's words as she wished. Then he paused a moment and said gently, "God bless you both," and went his way with a tear in his eye and a prayer in his heart, leaving them to their joy.

Soon after the culmination of Felicia's and Stephen's love story, a plan was worked out to bring to a climax the work that had been started in both Raymond and Chicago. Henry Maxwell came to Chicago with Rachel Winslow, Virginia Page, Rollin Page, Alexander Powers and President Marsh. The occasion was a remarkable gathering in the hall of the Settlement arranged by the bishop and Dr. Bruce.

There was invited into the Settlement Hall meeting that night men out of work, wretched creatures who had lost faith in God and man, anarchists and infidels, freethinkers and no thinkers. The representatives of the city's worst, most hopeless, dangerous, depraved elements faced Henry Maxwell and the other disciples when the meeting began.

And still the Holy Spirit moved through this selfish, pleasure-loving, sin-stained city. Every man and woman at the meeting that night had seen the Settlement motto over the door, blazing through the transparency set up by the divinity student: *What Would Jesus Do?*

When he first stepped through the doorway, Henry Maxwell was touched with deep emotion as he thought of the first time that question had come to him in the piteous appeal of the shabby young man who had appeared at the morning service in First Church.

Would the movement begun in Raymond actually spread over the country? He had come to Chicago with his friends, partly to see if the answer to that question would be found in the heart of a great city. In a few minutes he would face these people. He had grown strong and calm since he first spoke with trembling to that company of working men in the railroad shops; but now, as then, he breathed a deep prayer for help. Somehow he felt as if this meeting would expand the answer to his constant query, "What would Jesus do?"

23

When Henry Maxwell began to speak to the people crowded into the Settlement hall that night, it is doubtful if he had ever faced such an audience in his life. It is quite certain that the city of Raymond did not contain such a variety of humanity. Not even the Rectangle at its worst could furnish so many men and women who had fallen entirely out of the reach of the church and of all religious influence.

What would he talk about? He had already decided that point. He told, in the simplest language he could command, some of the results of obedience to the pledge as it had been taken in Raymond. Every man and woman in that audience knew something about Jesus Christ. They all had some idea of His character, and however much they had grown bitter toward the forms of Christian ecclesiasticism of the social system, they preserved some standard of right and truth; and what little some of them still retained was taken from the person of the Peasant of Galilee.

So they were interested in what Maxwell said about "What would Jesus do?" He began to apply the question to the social problem in general after finishing the story of Raymond. The audience was respectfully attentive. No, it was more than that. It was genuinely interested. As Mr. Maxwell went on, faces all over the hall leaned forward in an expectant manner seldom seen in staid church congregations. What would Jesus do?

Suppose that were the motto, Maxwell challenged them, not only of the churches but of the businessmen, the politicians, the newspapers, the working men, the society people. How long would it take, under such a standard of conduct, to revolutionize the world? What was the trouble with the world? It was suffering from selfishness. No one ever lived who had succeeded in overcoming selfishness like Jesus. If men followed Him, regardless of results, the world would at once begin to enjoy a new life.

Henry Maxwell never knew how much it meant to hold the respectful attention of that hall full of tormented and sinful humanity. The bishop and Dr. Bruce, sitting there looking on and seeing many faces that represented scorn of creeds, hatred of the social order, desperate narrowness and selfishness, marveled that even so soon under the influence of the Spirit the softening process had begun to lessen the bitterness of neglected and indifferent hearts.

And still, in spite of the outward show of respect to the speaker, no one, not even the bishop, had any true conception of the feelings pent-up in that room that night. Among the men who had heard of the meeting and responded to the invitation were twenty or thirty men out of work who had strolled past the Settlement that afternoon, read the notice of the meeting and come in out of curiosity and to escape the chill east wind.

It was a bitter night and the saloons were full. But in that whole district of over 30,000, the only door open to the people, with the exception of the saloons, was the clean, welcoming door of the Settlement. Where would a man without a home, work or friends naturally go, unless to the saloon?

It had been the custom at the Settlement for a free discussion to follow an open meeting of this kind. So when Mr. Maxwell finished and sat down, the bishop rose and announced that any man in the hall was at liberty to ask questions, to speak out his feelings or declare his convictions. There was always the understanding that whoever took part was to observe the simple rules that governed parliamentary bodies and obey the three-minute rule which, by common consent, would be enforced on account of the numbers present.

Instantly a number of voices from men who had attended previous meetings of this kind exclaimed, "Consent! Consent!"

The bishop sat down, and immediately a man near the middle of the hall arose and began to speak.

"I want to say that what Mr. Maxwell has said tonight comes pretty close to me. I knew Jack Manning, the fellow he told about, who died at his house. I worked next to him in a printer's shop in Philadelphia for two years. Jack was a good fellow. He loaned me five dollars once when I was in a hole and I never got a chance to pay him back. He moved to New York, owing to a change in the management of the office that threw him out, and I never saw him again.

"When the linotype machines came in, I was one of the men to go out just as he did. I have been out most of the time since. They say inventions are a good thing. I don't always see it myself. But I suppose I'm prejudiced. A man naturally is, when he loses a steady job because a machine takes his place.

"About this Christianity he tells about, it's all right. But I never expect to see any such sacrifice on the part of the church people. So far as my observation goes, they're just as selfish and greedy for money and worldly success as anybody. I except the bishop and Dr. Bruce and a few others. But I never found much difference between men of the world, as they're called, and church members when it came to business and moneymaking. One class is just as bad as another there."

Cries of *That's so*, *You're right!* and *Of course!* interrupted the speaker, and the minute he sat down two men jumped up and began to talk at once.

The bishop, calling them to order, indicated which was entitled to the floor. The man who remained standing began eagerly.

"This is the first time I was ever in here, and maybe it'll be the last. Fact is, I'm about at the end of my string. I've tramped this city for work until I'm sick. I have plenty of company. Say, I'd like to ask a question of the minister. May I?"

"By all means," replied Mr. Maxwell.

"This is my question." The man leaned forward and stretched out a long arm with dramatic effect.

"I want to know what Jesus would do in my case? I haven't had a stroke of work for two months. I've got a wife and three children, and I love them as much as I would if I were worth a million dollars. I've been living off a little earnings I saved up during the World's Fair jobs I got. I'm a carpenter by trade, and I've tried every way I know to get a job. You say we ought to take for our motto 'What would Jesus do?' What would He do if He were out of work like me?"

Mr. Maxwell sat staring at the great sea of faces all intent on his own, and no answer to this man's question seemed for the time being to be possible. *O God!* his heart prayed. *Is there any condition more awful than for a man in good health, able and eager to work but who is unable, to get nothing to do? What would Jesus do?*

All this and more did Henry Maxwell ponder for a moment. Then he spoke, "Is there any man in the room who is a Christian disciple who has been in this condition and has tried to do as Jesus would do? If so, such a man can answer this question better than I."

There was a moment's hush over the room. Then a man near the front of the hall slowly rose. He was an old man, and the hand he laid on the back of the bench in front of him trembled as he spoke.

"I think I can safely say that I have many times been in just such a condition and have always tried to be a Christian under all conditions. I don't know as I have always asked the question 'What would Jesus do?' when I have been out of work, but I do know I tried to be His disciple at all times.

"Yes," the man went on with a sad smile that appeared more pathetic to the bishop and Mr. Maxwell than the younger man's grim despair. "Yes, I have begged, and I have been to the charity institutions, and I have done everything when out of a job except steal and lie in order to get food and fuel. I don't know as Jesus would have done some of the things I have been obliged to do for a living. But I know I have never knowingly done wrong when out of work. Sometimes I think maybe he would have starved sooner than beg, but I don't know."

A silence followed, broken by a fierce voice from a large, black-haired, heavy-beaded man who sat three seats from the bishop. The minute he spoke, nearly every man in the hall leaned forward with anticipation.

"That's Carlsen, the socialist leader. Now you'll hear something," said one of the men in a loud whisper.

"This is all bosh to my mind," began Carlsen, while his great, bristling beard shook with a deep, inward anger. "The whole of our system is at fault. What we call civilization is rotten to the core. There is no use trying to hide it or cover it up. We live in an age of capitalistic greed that means death to thousands of innocent men, women, and children. I thank God, if there is a God—which I very much doubt—that I for one have never dared to marry and try to have a home.

"Home! Talk about hell! Is there any worse hell than this man, with his three children, has on his hands right this minute? And he's only one out of thousands. And yet this city, and every other big city in this country, has its thousands of professing Christians who have all the luxuries and comforts, and who go to church Sundays and sing their hymns about giving all to Jesus and bearing the cross and following Him all the way and being saved.

"I don't say that there aren't good men and women among them. But let the minister who has spoken to us here tonight go into any one of a dozen aristocratic churches I could name and propose to the members to take any such pledge as the one he's mentioned here tonight, and see how quick the people would laugh at him as a fool or a crank or a fanatic.

"No, that's not the remedy. That can't ever amount to anything. We've got to have a new start in the way of government. The whole thing needs reconstruction. I don't look for any reform worth anything to come out of the churches. They are not with the people. They are with the aristocrats, the men of money. The trusts and monopolies have their greatest men in the churches. The ministers as a class are their slaves. What we need is a system that will start from the common basis of socialism founded on the rights of the common people—"

Carlsen had evidently forgotten all about the three-minute rule, and was launching himself into a regular oration that meant, in his usual surroundings before his usual audience, an hour at least, when the man just behind him pulled him down unceremoniously and arose.

Carlsen was angry at first and threatened a little disturbance, but the bishop reminded him of the rule, so he subsided with several mutterings in his beard, while the next speaker began with a strong eulogy on the value of the single tax as a genuine remedy for all social ills. He was followed by a man who made a bitter attack on churches and ministers and declared that the two great obstacles to all true reform were the courts and the ecclesiastical machines.

When he sat down, a man who bore every mark of being a street laborer sprang to his feet and poured a perfect torrent of abuse against the corporations, especially the railroads. The minute his time was up, a big brawny fellow, who said he was a metal worker by trade, claimed the floor and declared that the remedy for the social wrongs was trade unionism. This, he said, would bring on the millennium for labor more surely than anything else. The next man endeavored to give some reasons why so many persons were out of work and condemned inventions as works of the devil. He was loudly applauded by the rest of the company.

Finally the bishop called time on the free-for-all and asked Rachel to sing.

When Rachel Winslow began to sing before this rough, noisy group, she had never prayed more deeply for results to come from her voice—the voice which she now regarded as the Master's, to be used for Him.

Certainly her prayer was being answered as she sang. She had chosen the words:

> Hark! The voice of Jesus calling:
> Follow me, follow me!

Again Henry Maxwell, sitting there, was reminded of his first night at the Rectangle in the tent when Rachel sang the people into quiet. The effect was the same now. Rachel's great natural ability entranced the men who had drifted in from the street. The song poured out through the hall as free and glad as if it were a foretaste of salvation itself.

Carlsen, with his great, black-bearded face uplifted, absorbed the music with the deep love of it peculiar to his nationality. A tear ran down his cheek and glistened in his beard, as his face softened and became almost noble in its aspect. The man out of work who wanted to know what Jesus would do in his place sat with a grimy hand on the back of the bench in front of him, with his mouth partly open, his great tragedy for the moment forgotten. The song, while it lasted, was food and work and warmth and union with his wife and babies once more.

The man who had spoken so fiercely against churches and ministers sat at first with his head erect and a look of stolid resistance, as if he stubbornly resented the introduction into the exercises of anything even remotely connected with the Church or its form of worship. But gradually he yielded to the power that was swaying the hearts of all persons in that room, and a look of sad thoughtfulness crept over his face.

The bishop thought that night, while Rachel was singing, that if the world of sinful, diseased, depraved, lost humanity could only have the Gospel preached to it by consecrated sopranos and professional tenors and altos and basses, he believed it would hasten the coming of the Kingdom quicker than any other one force.

Why, he cried in his heart as he listened, had the world's great treasure in song so often been held far from the poor, because the personal possessor of voice or fingers capable of stirring inspirational melody had so often regarded the gift as something with which to make money? Would there be no martyrs among the gifted ones of the earth? Would there be no giving of this great gift, as well as of others?

And Henry Maxwell, again as before, remembered that other audience at the Rectangle with increasing longing for a larger spread of the new discipleship. What he had seen and heard at the Settlement burned into him more deeply the belief that the problem of the city would be solved if the Christians in it should once follow Jesus as He gave commandment. But what of this great mass of neglected humanity, the very kind of humanity the Savior came to save, with all its mistakes and narrowness, its wretchedness and loss of hope, and above all its unqualified bitterness toward the Church? That was what smote him deepest.

Was the Church so far from the Master, then, that the people no longer found Him there? Was it true that the Church had lost its power over the very kind of humanity which in the early ages of Christianity it had reached in the greatest numbers?

Was it really true that big city churches, as a rule, would refuse to walk in Jesus's steps and sacrifice for his sake?

Henry Maxwell kept asking this last question even after Rachel had finished singing and the meeting had ended. He asked it while the little company of residents, along with the Raymond visitors, were having a devotional service, as was the custom in the Settlement. He asked it during a conference with the bishop and Dr. Bruce that lasted until one in the morning.

He asked it again as he knelt again before sleeping, and poured out his soul in a petition for spiritual baptism on the Church in America such as it had never known. He asked it the first thing in the morning and all through the day as he went over the Settlement district and saw the life of the people so far removed from the abundant life. Would church members—the Christians not only in the churches of Chicago but throughout the country—refuse to walk in His steps, if in order to do so they must actually take up a cross and follow Him?

This was the one question that continually demanded an answer.

He had planned when he came to the city to return to Raymond and be in his own pulpit on Sunday. But Friday morning he had received at the Settlement a call from the pastor of one of the largest churches in Chicago, inviting him to fill the pulpit Sunday morning and evening.

At first he hesitated, but finally accepted, seeing in it the hand of the Spirit's guiding power. He would test his own question. He would prove the truth or falsity of the charge made against the Church at the Settlement meeting. How far would it go in its self-denial for Jesus's sake? How close would it walk in His steps? Was the Church willing to suffer for its Master?

Maxwell spent nearly all of Saturday night in prayer. There had never been so great a wrestling in his soul, not even during his strongest experiences in Raymond. He had in fact entered upon another new experience. The definition of his own discipleship was receiving an added test at this time, and he was being led into a larger truth of his Lord.

24

Sunday morning the large Chicago church was filled to its utmost. Henry Maxwell, coming into the pulpit from that all-night vigil, felt the pressure of great curiosity on the part of the people. They had heard of the Raymond movement, as all the churches had, and the recent action of Dr. Bruce had added to the general interest in the pledge.

Along with this curiosity Mr. Maxwell sensed something deeper, more serious. And in the knowledge that the Spirit's presence was his living strength, he brought God's message to the church that day.

Henry Maxwell had always had a dramatic preaching style, but ever since he had promised to do as Jesus would do, he had grown in a certain quality of persuasiveness that had all the essentials of true eloquence. This morning the people felt the complete sincerity and humility of a man who had gone deep into the heart of a great truth.

After telling briefly of some results in his own church in Raymond since the pledge was taken, he went on to ask the question he had been asking since the Settlement meeting.

He took for his theme the story of the young man who came to Jesus, asking what he must do to obtain eternal life. Jesus had tested him: "Sell all that thou hast and give to the poor and thou shalt have treasure in heaven; and come, follow me." But the young man was not willing to suffer to that extent. If following Jesus meant suffering in that way, he was not willing. He would like to follow Jesus, but not if he had to give so much.

"Is it true," asked Henry Maxwell, his thoughtful face glowing, "that the Church of today, the Church that is called after Christ's own name, would refuse to follow Him at the expense of suffering and physical loss? At a large gathering in the Settlement last week, a leader of the working class stated that it was hopeless to look to the Church for any reform or redemption of society. On what was that statement based? Plainly on the assumption that the Church contains, for the most part, men and women who think more of their own ease and luxury than of the sufferings and needs and sins of humanity.

"How true is that assumption? Are the Christians of America ready to have their discipleship tested? How about the men who possess large wealth? Are they ready to take that wealth and use it as Jesus would? How about the men and women of great talent? Are they ready to consecrate that talent to humanity, as Jesus undoubtedly would do?

Is it not true that the call has come in this age for a new exhibition of Christian discipleship? You who live in this great, sinful city must know that better than I do. Is it possible you can go your ways careless or thoughtless of the awful condition of men and women and children who are dying, body and soul, for need of Christian help? Is it not a matter of concern to you personally that the saloon kills its thousands more surely than war? Is it not a matter of personal suffering in some form for you that thousands of able-bodied, willing men tramp the streets of this city, and all cities, crying for work and drifting into crime and suicide because they cannot find it? Can you say that this is none of your business?

"What is the test of Christian discipleship? Is it not the same as in Christ's own lifetime? Have our surroundings modified or changed the test? If Jesus were here today, would He not call some of the members of this very church to do just what He commanded the rich young man, and ask them to give up their wealth and literally follow Him? I believe He would do that if He felt certain that any church member thought more of his possessions than of his Savior. The test would be the same today as then.

"I believe Jesus would demand as close a following, as great a denial of self, as when He lived in person on the earth and said, 'Except a man renounceth all that he hath, he cannot be my disciple.' That is, unless a man is willing to do that for Jesus's sake, he cannot be Jesus's disciple.

"What would happen," continued Mr. Maxwell, "if in this city every church member should begin to do as Jesus would do? It staggers our minds to imagine the results! We all know that certain things would be impossible that are now practiced by church members. What would Jesus do in the matter of wealth? How would He spend it? How would

Jesus be governed in the making of money? Would He take rentals from saloons? From tenement property?

"What would Jesus do about the great army of unemployed who tramp the streets and curse the church, or are indifferent to it, lost in the bitter struggle for the bread that tastes bitter when it is earned on account of the desperate conflict to get it? Would He say it was none of His business?

"What would Jesus do in the center of a civilization that hurries so fast after money that the girls employed in great business houses are not paid enough to keep soul and body together without fearful temptations? Where the demands of trade sacrifice hundreds of lads in a business that ignores all Christian duties toward them in the way of education and moral training and personal affection? Would Jesus, if he were here today as a part of our age and commercial industry, feel nothing, do nothing, say nothing in the face of these facts that every businessman knows?

"Does the Church do its duty in following Jesus when it gives so little money to establish missions or relieve extreme cases of want? Is it any sacrifice for a man who is worth ten million dollars simply to give ten thousand dollars for some benevolent work? Is he not giving something that costs him practically nothing so far as any personal pain or suffering goes? Is it true that the Christian disciples today in most of our churches are living soft, selfish lives, very far from any sacrifice that can be called sacrifice? What would Jesus do?

"It is the personal element that Christian discipleship needs to emphasize. 'The gift without the giver is bare.' The call of this age is a call for a new discipleship, a new following of Jesus, more like the early, simple, apostolic Christianity when the disciples left all and literally followed the Master. Nothing but a discipleship of this kind can face the destructive selfishness of the age, with any hope of overcoming it. Then it would be possible to sing with the exact truth:

> Jesus, I my cross have taken,
> All to leave and follow thee.

"If we can sing that truly, then we may claim discipleship. But if our definition of being a Christian is simply to enjoy the privileges of worship, be generous at no expense to ourselves, have a good, easy time surrounded by pleasant friends and by comfortable things, live respectably, and at the same time avoid the world's great stress of sin and trouble because it is too painful—if this is our definition of Christianity, then surely we are a long way from following the steps of Him who trod the way with tears of anguish for a lost humanity; who sweat, as it were, great drops of blood; who cried out on the upreared cross, 'My God! My God! Why hast thou forsaken me'!"

When Henry Maxwell finished his sermon, a great silence fell over the congregation. Through the silence, there came to those present a consciousness of the presence of a divine Power. Everyone expected the preacher to call for volunteers who would do as Jesus would do. But Maxwell had been led by the Spirit to deliver his message and wait for results.

He closed the service with a prayer, and the people slowly began to move out of their pews.

Then followed a scene that could never have happened if Maxwell had attempted to rally these people to a cause without the leading of the Holy Spirit.

Men and women in great numbers crowded around the platform to see Mr. Maxwell and to bring him the promise of their consecration to the pledge to do as Jesus would do. It was a voluntary, spontaneous movement that broke upon his soul with a result he could not measure.

But had he not been praying for this very thing? It was an answer that more than met his desires.

The people staying after the service then met in a prayer service that in many ways repeated the Raymond experience. In the evening, to Mr. Maxwell's joy, the Endeavor Society—almost to a member—came forward as so many of the church members had done in the morning and seriously, solemnly, took the pledge to do as Jesus would do. A deep wave of spiritual baptism broke over the meeting near its close that was indescribable in its tender, joyful, sympathetic results.

That was a remarkable day in the history of that church, but even more so in the history of Henry Maxwell. He left the meeting very late. He went to his room at the Settlement where he was still staying, and after an hour with the bishop and Dr. Bruce, which was spent in a joyful rehearsal of the wonderful events of the day, he sat down to think over again, by himself, all the experience he was having as a Christian disciple.

He knelt to pray, as he always did before going to sleep, and while he was on his knees he had a waking vision of what a wonderful world there could be once the new discipleship had made its way into the conscience and conscientiousness of Christendom. He was fully awake, but what he saw distinctly was a series of future events—a vision planted in his heart and mind and soul by his Creator.

He saw himself going back to First Church in Raymond, living there in a simpler, more self-denying fashion than he had yet been willing to live, because he saw ways in which he could help others really dependent on him for help. He also saw, more dimly, that the time would come when his position as pastor of the church would cause him to suffer more on account of growing opposition to his interpretation of Jesus and His conduct.

But this was vaguely outlined. Through it all he heard the words *My grace is sufficient for thee.*

He saw Rachel Winslow and Virginia Page going on with their work of service at the Rectangle and reaching out loving hands of helpfulness far beyond the limits of Raymond. Rachel he saw married to Rollin Page, both fully consecrated to the Master's use, both following His steps with an eagerness intensified and purified by their love for each other. And Rachel's voice sang on in the slums and dark places of despair and sin, drawing lost souls back to God.

He saw President Marsh of the college using his vast learning and influence to bring reform in city politics and to inspire young men and women to live lives of Christian service, always teaching them that the educated have more responsibility for the weak and ignorant.

He saw Alexander Powers meeting with sore trials in his family life, with a constant sorrow in the estrangement of wife and friends, but still going his way in all honor, serving in all his strength the Master whom he had obeyed even unto loss of social distinction and wealth.

He saw Milton Wright, the merchant, meeting with great reverses that fell through a combination of circumstances no fault of his own, but coming out of his reverses with Christian honor to begin again, and work up to a position where he could be an example to hundreds of young men of what Jesus would do in business.

He saw Edward Norman, editor of the *News*, creating a new approach in journalism that would in time come to be recognized as one of the strong forces of the nation. His would be the first of a series of such papers begun and carried on by other disciples who had also taken the pledge.

He saw Jasper Chase, who had denied his Master, moving into a cold, cynical life, writing novels that were social successes, but each one with a sting in it, the reminder of his denial.

He saw Rose Sterling, dependent for some years upon her aunt and Felicia, finally married to a man far older than herself, accepting the burden of a relationship that had no love in it on her part, because of her desire to be the wife of a rich man and enjoy the physical luxuries that were all of life to her. Over this life the vision cast certain dark shadows that were not shown in detail.

He saw Felicia and Stephen Clyde happily married, living a joyful life together, enthusiastically pouring out their great strong service into the dull, dark, terrible places of Chicago, and redeeming souls through the personal touch of their home dedicated to the human sickness all about them.

He saw Dr. Bruce and Bishop Hampton going on with the Settlement work. He seemed to see the great blazing motto over the door enlarged: *What Would Jesus Do?* And by this motto everyone who entered the Settlement walked in the steps of the Master.

He saw Burns and his companion and a great company of men like them, redeemed and giving in turn to others, conquering their passions by divine grace and proving by their daily lives the reality of rebirth, even in the lowest and most abandoned of persons.

And then he saw the figure of the Son of God beckoning to him and to all the other actors in his life history. An angel choir somewhere was singing. There was sound as of many voices and a shout as of a great victory. And the figure of Jesus grew more and more splendid. He stood at the end of a long flight of steps.

"O my Master, has the time come for a new dawn of Christian activity? O my Lord, break upon the Christendom of this age with Your light and truth! Help us to follow Thee all the way!"

Mr. Maxwell arose at last with the awe of one who has looked at heavenly things. He felt the human forces and sins of the world as never before. And with a hope that walks hand-in-hand with faith and love, Henry Maxwell, disciple of Jesus, lay down to sleep and dreamed of the regeneration of Christendom, and saw in his dream a Church of Jesus Christ "without spot or wrinkle or any such thing," following Him all the way, walking obediently in His steps.